BREE

Shelly

Tomoko

Jules

Kenzie

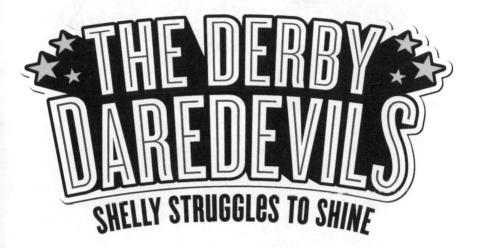

SHELLY STRUGGLES TO SHINE

BY KIT ROSEWATER

ILLUSTRATED BY
SOPHIE ESCABASSE

AMULET BOOKS
NEW YORK

Cataloging-in-Publication Data has been applied for and may be obtained from the Library of Congress.

ISBN 978-1-4197-4685-7

Text copyright © 2020 Christyl Rosewater
Illustrations copyright © 2020 Sophie Escabasse
Book design by Marcie Lawrence

Printed and bound in U.S.A.
10 9 8 7 6 5 4 3 2

ABRAMS The Art of Books
195 Broadway, New York, NY 10007
abramsbooks.com

For Cymeon, who drew the first "squiggle" of my
life as a writer. Thanks, Mom.
—K.R.

CHAPTER ONE

"THEY HAVE TO BE HERE. THEY CAN'T *NOT* BE HERE!"

Fifth grader Shelly Baum leaned across the counter. She used her freshly licked-clean ice pop stick to point toward a pile of skates in the back corner.

"There. With the tangled laces. Those are mine."

The woman behind the counter, known as Pearl Jammer on the roller derby track, turned toward the pile.

"Those haven't been cleaned yet," Pearl Jammer said.

Shelly sent a dragon breath of exasperation through her nostrils. "But I just wore them yesterday! If they smell like feet, it's *my* feet!"

Pearl Jammer sighed and fished out the pair of old roller skates like a magician pulling a rabbit from a hat. Shelly could even see the bunny ear squiggle in the long, looping laces.

"These?"

"Yep!" Shelly grinned. Her fingers fluttered as she reached for the skates. She checked for the spot of yellow paint on the back wheel, just to be sure.

Shelly slipped her feet into the worn leather, then tugged and twisted and pulled the laces taut around her ankles.

"You ready?" Shelly asked. She turned over her shoulder.

Kenzie, Shelly's best friend, plopped down on the bleachers next to Shelly. She stuffed her feet into her own pair of skates and took one last bite of her Sour Birthday ice pop—the Dynamic Duo's favorite. Sour Birthday was a mix of birthday cake and vinegar flavors. It was a little sweet, a little sour, and a whole lot of wacky, which was a pretty good way to describe Shelly and Kenzie.

"Ready," Kenzie said as she clipped on her helmet.

The girls bumped fists and slid onto the track for their usual warm-up. They had been going to Free Skate nights together at the Austin roller derby warehouse ever since they were in third grade. It had been a Dynamic Duo tradition until last month, when something incredible happened.

"Wait up!"

Tomoko waved from the side of the rink. Shelly and Kenzie stopped in unison.

"Hey!" Shelly said.

Tomoko pumped her arms until she was skating next to the others.

A month ago, Shelly and Kenzie decided to turn their Dynamic Duo into a group of awesome skaters. Now, instead of practicing just with Kenzie, Shelly got to work on even more derby moves!

Shelly let Tomoko and Kenzie get in front of her, then tried to zigzag between them to pass. Tomoko sprang across the track, switching her hips back and forth to keep Shelly behind her.

"Jeez, Tomoko, you're too good!" Shelly said. She brushed the sweat from her forehead.

"Best blocker on the team!" Kenzie said. She nudged Tomoko and smiled.

"What's that about best on the team?"

Bree, another member of the girls' new group, shot across the track and nudged Kenzie's side.

"Hey friends."

"Hey Bree," Shelly said. "Don't worry, we're talking about blocking, not jamming. You're still the fastest."

Bree grinned and shot around the track, doing a whole extra lap around the others. She quickly caught up with the team again.

Tomoko shook her head. "It's like you have turbo jets in your skates!"

Bree laughed. The four skaters clustered together, swerving around the corner by the front entrance.

"Hi-yah!"

Jules, the smallest and fiercest of the bunch, hopped onto the track and chopped the air in front of her as she made her way to the rest.

Shelly looked at Kenzie and beamed. Not long ago, Tomoko, Bree, and Jules were nearly strangers. But now the five girls made up the Derby Daredevils, the raddest team in the Austin, Texas, junior roller derby league!

Kenzie held up a hand.

"Let's practice!"

Bree slipped behind the others and waited. Shelly, Kenzie, Tomoko, and Jules skated close together as the pack of blockers. Once the pack was half a lap ahead, Bree *clack-clack-clack-*ed around the track. As the Daredevils' jammer, Bree's job was to speed ahead and slip through the pack.

Shelly listened as Bree came up from behind. While Bree worked on speed, Shelly and the other blockers practiced different moves to block the opposing team's jammer and help Bree zoom through the pack. They had a list of game plays, which were pretty risky and only worked half the time. But the Daredevils were known for taking risks on the track.

"The Flying Circle of Doom," Kenzie whispered.

Shelly, Tomoko, and Jules nodded. Kenzie was a great strategizer. She planned all of the team's best game plays.

"OK," Kenzie said. "Get in formation!"

Shelly tightened her fists and bent her knees, just like she always did. Maybe she wasn't the best blocker, or the best planner, or the fastest, or the fiercest . . . but she definitely knew how to hold her ground.

"Ahhhhh!"

A squeaky voice sailed out of nowhere. Shelly's knees buckled as a little kid crashed into her left leg. She wobbled back and forth.

"W-whoa," Shelly said.

Two older boys zoomed past on either side. Shelly felt like she was in a wind tunnel. She leaned one way, then the other, then—

CRASH!

Shelly dropped onto her knees and rolled to the side of the rink. The team broke formation and surrounded her.

"Dude," Jules said, "that was a really good fall. And I should know. I fall *a lot*."

"Thanks," Shelly groaned. She let Jules help her off the track. "Sorry I lost my balance."

"It's not your fault," Kenzie said. "We shouldn't be practicing during Free Skate anyway."

The rest of the team stepped off of the track behind Shelly.

"Dumb guys out there," Bree said, "getting close to other skaters and freaking them out. They treat people like traffic cones."

Shelly nodded. If only those skaters knew what it was like to take a hip check on the track! She reached inside her bag and grabbed a pencil.

"Skating around little kids is hard too," Tomoko pointed out. She leaned over Shelly's shoulder. "Hey, what's that?"

Shelly had her sketchbook open on her lap. She drew Kenzilla—Kenzie's super-cool derby persona—with giant scaly skates shaped like dinosaur feet.

"That's awesome!" Jules said. "You can show her stomping on all the other Free Skaters who knock into us."

Shelly smiled and drew stick figures skidding and sliding away.

Kenzie pinned her elbows to her sides and wagged her hips as she stomped in front of the bleachers.

"ROAR!"

The Daredevils broke into laughter.

"Perfect," Bree said. "You gotta use that move in our next derby jam."

"I thought I heard derby talk."

The girls all twisted their heads toward the snack stand. Mambo Rambo, a junior league coach, stepped around the corner holding a bag of kettle corn.

"What's the point of Free Skate night?" Jules asked. "Just change it to an extra derby practice. Boom, every-one's happy."

"Everyone?" Mambo swept her arm over the track. "Don't forget the skaters outside of derby. They deserve to have their moment too."

Mambo took a seat on the bleachers next to Shelly. She smiled at Shelly's picture, then turned to the whole group.

"Y'all are looking pretty good out there," she said. "Though, Jules, make sure you don't swing your arms around. In a bout, that's a penalty. You'll end up sitting in the box."

"What's the box?" Shelly asked.

"It's what happens when you break a rule," Mambo said.

She looked at Jules. "Like striking with an arm. So stick to hip checks."

Bree placed a hand on her hip. "Are bouts coming soon?" she asked.

The Daredevils had been talking nonstop about bouts, the name for official derby games, ever since tryouts. They had lost their tryout scrimmage against the Cherry Pits, another team in the league. Shelly and the others were hungry for a rematch.

Mambo gave a sympathetic smile. "I'm afraid bout season is on hold," she said. "But you'll see why soon." She paused for a moment, then stood and left the bleachers.

The Daredevils were silent until Mambo disappeared around the corner. They leaned into a huddle.

"Did she . . . wink at us?" Bree asked.

Kenzie nodded. "Yep. That was definitely a wink."

"What do you think's going on?" Tomoko said.

Jules rubbed her hands together. "Something good, I hope."

"Me too," Shelly said. She glanced toward the snack bar and grinned.

The derby coaches had something up their sleeves.

CHAPTER TWO

THE NEXT MORNING, SHELLY'S MOM WALKED HER TO roller derby practice. Her mom carried a paint-splattered satchel over her shoulder and had a pencil tucked behind one ear. Shelly ran ahead with her backpack, leaping across the sidewalk and bounding from bike racks to drain covers.

"Playing the hot lava game?" her mom called.

Shelly paused on a sewer grate. "Uh-huh. I'm stuck, though. There's lava all the way from here to that stop sign."

"Hmmm." Shelly's mom took the pencil from behind her ear and drew an invisible line through the air. "Good news! I just made a bridge for you to cross over."

"Thanks, Mom!"

Shelly hopped off the grate and onto the bridge.

The satchel bumped Shelly's side as her mom caught up to her.

"Another class today?" Shelly asked, eyeing the canvas bag.

Her mom nodded. "Uh-huh. Sundays and Tuesdays. You want to drop in this week?"

Shelly tapped her chin. Her mom taught sculpture classes at the community art center. Whenever Shelly visited, her mom always set up a station for her. But sculpting actual objects was hard for Shelly. She was much better at coming up with flat pictures in her sketchbook.

"OK," Shelly said. She definitely liked seeing what all the other artists in the class were up to. Fen always made the coolest sculptures. And Mrs. Otterloo sometimes even brought strawberry hard candies, which no one else wanted except for Shelly.

"Great," her mom said. "I'll see you Tuesday. Tell your dad hi for me!"

They turned the corner to the derby warehouse. Shelly could see Bree and Tomoko chatting in the parking lot. She started to race toward them.

"Love you!" her mom called.

Shelly's heels dug into the concrete. She made a U-turn and came crashing back into her mom's side.

"Love you too," Shelly said. She U-turned again and

leaped over puddles of lava until she met Bree and Tomoko by the front doors.

"It's Bomb Shell!" they yelled. That was Shelly's derby name. Shelly jumped into the air and splayed out her arms.

"Kablooey!" she said. The girls all laughed.

They went inside and threw on their gear, then joined Kenzie and Jules on the track. The Daredevils didn't work on their secret formations in regular roller derby practice. The coaches—Mambo Rambo, Look Out, and Razzle Dazzle—kept all five teams busy with drills and exercises.

Shelly skated between Kenzie and Tomoko. She watched the other skaters as they glided over the rink. Could she make a skate in her mom's class? Shelly shook her head. What good was a skate made out of clay? She would probably just watch the others and doodle like she always did. She could finish her sketch of Kenzilla and add tiny buildings in the background for Kenzie to knock over.

Fffttt!

Razzle Dazzle blew a whistle.

"Backward bubbles! Let's go!"

Suddenly the rink full of skaters slowed to a stop. One by one, players started wiggling and moving backward. Jules fell over right away, which was not so unusual for her. Shelly held out an arm.

"You OK?" Shelly asked.

"Yep!" Jules said. She grasped on to Shelly's hand and shot back up again.

Shelly moved her skates out and brought them together. Moved them out, brought them together.

"Hey, you're getting pretty good!" Bree said, looking at Shelly's skates.

"How do you do that so smooth?" Kenzie asked.

"I pretend I'm drawing circles with my skates," Shelly said. "And each skate is a pencil. So you go out, like this—"

She moved her skates out wide. "—then you bring them in."

Shelly pushed her toes in, pulling her heels close. Kenzie and Tomoko studied Shelly's skates as they practiced beside her. Shelly's cheeks flushed—she almost never got to be the expert of a skating drill.

The team did two whole laps of backward bubbles before the whistle blew again.

Fffttt!

"Crossover time!" Raz called out. "Take it nice and slow. Give each other some space."

The Daredevils spread out across the track. Every time Shelly looped around a curve, she did her best to lift one skate up and cross it over the other. It was so hard to keep her balance!

Oof!

Shelly looked to her side. Kenzie tripped over her skate and went down by the railing.

"Nice fall, Kenzilla!" Coach Look Out called. "Way to land safely. Let's bring in it, folks. To the jammer line!"

Shelly waited for Kenzie, then skated over to a strip of thick red tape across the track. This was where Bree stood as jammer whenever the girls played scrimmages. Sometimes Shelly had to stand here when she practiced jamming during drills. It was also the main gathering spot for the league. All five teams took a knee in front of the coaches.

"Excellent crossovers out there," Mambo said. "Y'all are really working on your balance and control. Your roller derby toolbox is filling up."

"When do we get to use those tools, though?" one player asked.

Shelly and the rest of the Daredevils glanced at the player. It was Molly, the jammer from the Cherry Pits.

"Yeah," another player said. "It's a-*bout* time! Get it?"

Mambo and the other coaches laughed.

"We get it," Mambo said. "Trust us."

Shelly squinted at Mambo. She had that twinkle in her eye again.

"We won't be playing local bouts for another few weeks. But Raz and Lo and I have something extra special planned for the league in the meantime."

Everyone leaned forward.

"What is it?" a girl asked.

Raz cleared her throat. "A chance to practice against some new teams."

"You mean like official teams?" Bree asked.

"Not adult teams," Lo said. "But a junior league from New Mexico is coming through Austin next week, and they'd like to play some roller derby with us! How would y'all feel about a tournament next weekend?"

WOOOOO!

If the warehouse had a noise meter, the dial would be cranked to ten. The skaters all broke into shouts and cheers.

"This is going to be awesome!" Jules cried. "Awesome awesome awesome!"

Jules popped up and danced in circles over the jammer line. She spun around and smacked the air like she was playing an invisible drum set. Shelly and the other Daredevils jumped up behind Jules and started dancing too. Shelly waved her

arms like they were made of jelly. She shook her hips from side to side.

"All right, all right." Mambo clapped her hands to get everyone's attention. "Seeing as how your focus is scattering faster than a dropped bowl of ants, we'll let you spend the last fifteen minutes of practice grouping with your teams. Don't forget, you'll need to coordinate your team look, and it won't hurt to come up with some jam strategies."

Shelly turned and shared a grin with Kenzie. If there was one thing the Daredevils had down, it was strategy.

CHAPTER THREE

SHELLY PLUCKED HER SKETCHBOOK OUT OF HER backpack and skated after the others.

"Wait up!" she called.

The five Daredevils settled together in a corner of the warehouse, far away from the other four teams. Shelly opened the book to a blank page and hovered her pencil over it.

"This is great news," Kenzie said. "We'll get to show off our secret formations at a real tournament!"

"We'll have to practice extra hard this week," Jules said. "Like, live and breathe derby."

Tomoko clapped her hands. "The sun's going down later, so we can stay longer at the park!"

Bree pointed at her. "Excellent. Every day after school, meet at the park for off-skates workouts."

"Maybe we can use the basketball court behind the warehouse on Friday," Kenzie said. "For an on-skates workout too. We can practice our plays like the Flying Circle of Doom and the Crying Banshee. You writing this all down, Bomb Shell?"

"Uh-huh," Shelly said. Her pencil swirled over the page as she drew herself, Kenzie, Tomoko, and Jules hovering in a circle around Bree. Tiny pairs of bat wings stuck out from the girls' T-shirts.

"What's that?" Bree asked.

"It's us doing the Flying Circle of Doom!" Shelly said. She tapped her pencil on the bat wings. "Wouldn't it be awesome if we really could fly?"

"Oh yeah!" Jules said. She flapped her arms and screeched.

The other teams whipped their heads around and stared as the Daredevils laughed. Shelly made her notebook flap alongside Jules. As the chuckles died down, Tomoko wiped her eyes and leaned forward.

"So what should we do during the off-skates workouts?" Tomoko asked.

Kenzie leaned her chin in her hand. "Hmm. We'll want to work on speed and stuff. But more than just that."

"We can work on jumping," Jules suggested. "To avoid hitting anyone who falls on the track!"

Shelly nodded and flipped her sketchbook to a new page.

"I can bring some of those field cones from my house," Bree said.

Kenzie snapped her fingers. "Perfect. An obstacle course! We can build different ones and practice going through them!" Kenzie paused and glanced at Shelly.

"Um . . . those don't look like notes."

Shelly turned her notebook around so the others could

see. "They're jumpy skates! See the slinky springs at the bottom? We'd be able to touch the tops of trees!"

Tomoko and Bree laughed. Shelly twisted her drawing even closer to Kenzie, who offered a smile.

"It's a great picture," Kenzie said. "I was just hoping you could write down the stuff we're saying too."

"Oh." Shelly's shoulders hunched. Even though Kenzie was smiling, Shelly felt like she was in trouble.

Ffftttt!

Razzle Dazzle waved her arms. "That's time, teams! We'll see you here next week!"

The Daredevils pushed themselves to standing, then shuffled to their regular bench and undid their laces. They were back to talking about the off-skates workouts again.

"Tomoko should set up the blocking drills," Kenzie said. "Bree can help us with speed work. Jules can lead the hip-check practice."

"What about me?" Shelly asked. Her voice felt shy.

Kenzie furrowed her brow, thinking. "You can lead anything, really! Just come up with something this week, and you can be the leader."

"OK," Shelly said. She was a little sad Kenzie didn't have an answer right away.

Everyone knew Tomoko was a good blocker, and Bree was fast, and Jules good at hip checks, and Kenzie the planner . . . but what was Shelly's big role? Suddenly her funny drawings didn't seem like enough. She crumpled the pictures of bouncy skates and bat wings in her head, balling them into a thick seed of worry.

The light zinged off the warehouse doors as Shelly and the others left practice. Shelly's dad stood waving from the corner of the parking lot.

"See ya, Bomb Shell," Kenzie said.

"Later, Kenzilla," Shelly said. Her backpack *thunk-thunk-thunk*ed against her as she hopped to her dad.

"How's my favorite kiddo?" he asked, leaning over and scooping Shelly up.

Shelly's dad was tall and wiry. He was one of the strongest people Shelly knew, though she wasn't sure where he kept all his muscles.

"Good," Shelly said. She giggled a little. Her dad always had a way of making her laugh.

He set her down and lifted the backpack from her shoulders.

"You ready for home?"

Shelly nodded. She followed her dad toward the other side of the warehouse, away from the direction she and her mom had walked earlier.

They turned off of South Congress Avenue, passing by houses with beautiful green lawns and shutters painted in bright colors. They passed by Shelly's favorite yard, which had a magnolia tree with giant gold and silver ornaments that hung year-round. They passed by the place with the twin poodles that loved to bark, and the house made of shipping containers, and the front yard with a chicken coop and a sign that said: PET THE CHICKENS!

Once they passed by all the usual spots (and said hello to the chickens), Shelly and her dad arrived at a tiny house on the corner. The house sat over its own garage, with a staircase leading to the door.

Shelly and her dad clomped up the steps. Shelly patted the cow-shaped mailbox next to the door while her dad turned the key.

"Oh boy," her dad said once they were inside. He slipped off the backpack and sank onto the couch. "What a walk. I'm beat."

Shelly sank down next to him.

"You didn't even go to derby practice," Shelly said. "I had to work on backward bubbles and crossovers and one, two falls and *then* walk home."

"Crossovers, huh?" Shelly's dad said. "You mean like the ones in basketball?"

Shelly wrinkled her forehead.

"I don't think so. Crossovers are when we put one skate over the other."

"That seems simple enough." Shelly's dad caught her glare. "But I'll bet it's harder than it looks," he added quickly.

"Way harder," Shelly said. "I fall over half the time!"

"Uh-huh," her dad said. He leaped up and got two bottles of fizzy water from the kitchen. He held a bottle out to Shelly.

"For the hardworking athlete," he said.

Shelly took a huge gulp from her bottle. She let the tiny bubbles jump and dance inside her belly. She sighed happily. This was the taste of being with her dad.

"What are you working on this week?" Shelly asked.

Her dad took a swig of his water and wiped his mouth.

"You wanna see?" His eyebrows wiggled up and down. "Come on back."

Shelly followed him down the hall, past her small bedroom, through his room, and onto the tiny balcony looking over the backyard. They crept down a second set of rickety steps until they stood outside the garage, right in front of the side door.

"Take a gander," her dad said. He cracked the door open.

Shelly watched the afternoon light spill onto a flat metal slab shaped like the Texas longhorn, a cow with long, curving horns. The sign was painted rusty orange, the same color as the jerseys on the Austin college football team. The long-horn cow was their mascot.

"Wow," Shelly said. "It's huge. Where's this one going?"

"A restaurant over on Sixth Street," her dad said proudly. He rapped the sign with his knuckles. The metal billowed and rumbled like thunder.

Shelly looked around her dad's workshop. There were sharp scraps of metal everywhere, with tools set out on benches, bottles of polish on the floor, and paint cans lining the walls. Her dad could cut and bend metal into almost any shape under the sun. But no matter when Shelly peeked into his workshop, she always saw at least a few longhorns lying around.

"You like sports, right, Dad?"

Shelly's dad laughed. "Course I do. I started playing basketball when I was around your age."

"Really?" Shelly asked. She paused. "Who were you on the team?"

Her dad raised an eyebrow. "Not sure I follow."

Shelly folded her arms. "Like . . . what did you do? Were you the fast one? Or the mean one?"

Shelly's dad laughed. "I was the shiny one!" he said. "At least that's what my teammates called me. Come on, let's watch the sky turn."

He closed the door and bolted the lock. Shelly cocked her head. Shiny seemed like a strange name for her dad.

They climbed the steps back up to the balcony. Shelly's dad brought some chairs out from the corner. The two sat down and kicked their feet up on the railing.

"How come they called you Shiny?" Shelly asked.

Her dad leaned forward. "From all the medals I won," he said, grinning. "Placed in every tournament I went to! Took home trophies to show your granny. I even got my picture in the newspaper a few times."

"The real newspaper?" Shelly asked. Her eyes widened.

"The real deal," her dad said. He folded his arms over his lap and stared out into the evening. "I liked the nickname," he said finally. "Sure, it sounded silly. But those guys were glad to have me on the team. Your old dad used to be a basketball-slinging star."

Shelly's dad winked, and it was like night had sprung up on them right then, sliding through the branches all sneaky. Shelly realized she hadn't watched the sky turn. She had been too busy listening to her dad.

She looked over the yard as fireflies rose from the long grass, blinking like sputtering candles.

"A star," Shelly whispered.

The seed of worry in her head sparked into a seed of an idea.

CHAPTER FOUR

THE NEIGHBORHOOD BUSTLED WITH SOUNDS AS SHELLY walked to school the next morning. She could hear the hum of her dad's saw in the garage behind her, slicing into metal that would soon become another longhorn-shaped sign. A gardening crew had pulled up outside of a house farther down the block. Their leaf blowers and lawn mowers roared. The chickens clucked in their pen. The twin poodles barked and yipped.

Meanwhile, Shelly's mind was bustling too. She swung her backpack around to the front and pulled her sketchbook out. Drawing things she could see in her head was easy enough. Shelly could turn a circle into a roller skate wheel without thinking. But half-formed ideas were harder to pin down.

She grabbed the pencil she sometimes kept behind her

ear, just like her mom, and let the lead swirl across the paper. She drew herself in derby gear, flying high above the track while her teammates skated below. Constellations sprouted from the backs of her skates.

Shelly studied her drawing, squinting so the stars on the page almost seemed to twinkle. She wished she really did have flying skates. How else could she stand out in such a great team?

Shelly tucked her pencil back behind her ear and closed her sketchbook. She spread her arms wide and skipped and soared to school, imagining wearing shooting stars on her feet.

The sounds of chickens clucking were soon replaced with

kids chatting as they scurried through the front doors of Curie Elementary. Shelly dipped through the crowd and found Kenzie standing outside her locker.

"Hey Zilla," Shelly said.

Kenzie looked up from her phone, then smiled and tucked it away into her pack. The girls bumped fists and pretended to spit over their shoulders, their signature Dynamic Duo handshake. Whenever they were outside, they really did spit. Shelly had worked on her loogie technique forever before she got it just right.

"Hey Bomb Shell," Kenzie said. "You ready for practice today? Bree's leading."

"Cool," Shelly said. If Bree was leading, that probably meant a lot of running. Shelly still didn't know what she would do when it was her turn to lead the group.

Kenzie and Shelly ducked across the hall into the bathroom—the Daredevils' morning meeting spot. The girls stood in front of the sink and made faces at each other in the mirror.

"Oh, no! It's the hundred-foot-tall Kenzilla!"

"Rawwwrrr!" Kenzie clawed at the mirror. "Everyone get down! Bomb Shell's coming!"

"Boom!" Shelly said, tossing her arms out.

The toilet flushed. Kenzie and Shelly held their poses

perfectly still as Camila, another fifth grader and former Daredevils member, emerged from the stall. Camila didn't seem at all surprised to be washing her hands next to a lizard girl and a human firework.

"See you later," Camila said.

"See you, Camila!" Shelly called back.

The door swished closed. Kenzie and Shelly dropped their poses and laughed. Shelly hugged her notebook to her chest.

Kenzie patted some water on her head to smooth down her hair. "Make any new funny drawings lately?"

"Um . . . not really," Shelly said. She thought about the picture of her flying over the others. Usually she showed Kenzie all her drawings, but this one felt like it belonged only to her. "No funny stuff."

Kenzie turned the faucet off and shrugged. "OK."

Shelly paused. She thought of her dad's nickname back when he was a kid. Shelly didn't just want to make funny drawings anymore. She wanted to be important to the team.

Should she tell Kenzie what was on her mind?

The door squeaked open. Both Kenzie and Shelly turned away from the mirror as Tomoko and Jules stepped inside. Since Bree went to another school, this was about as complete as the Daredevils could get at Curie.

"It's the Tomonater!" Kenzie called.

Tomoko grinned. "Oh yeah, that name's feeling good. I can't wait to wear it on the track."

Shelly looked back and forth between the two. "You picked a derby name? When?"

Tomoko shrugged. "Right after you left with your dad. It came to me like a bolt of lightning. WHAM!" She smacked her palms together.

Shelly and Kenzie laughed. Shelly propped her sketchbook open on her knee. It was the first time any of the new members had come up with a derby name, and Shelly *had* to document it properly. She stretched her arm toward Tomoko, holding her pencil like a line.

"What are you doing?" Tomoko asked.

"Measuring," Shelly said. She dropped her arm back by her side. "OK, I actually don't know how it works. But I see my mom doing it all the time when she's sketching a model."

"Model?" Tomoko struck a pose. She turned to the side, then looked at Shelly over her shoulder. "How's this?"

"Perfect," Shelly said. She huddled close to the pages as she drew a picture of Tomoko with lights and buttons up and down her leggings so she looked like a killer robot. She drew glasses over Tomoko's eyes to make them look like one big laser.

The Tomonater! Shelly wrote underneath.

"That's wicked awesome!" Kenzie said.

Tomoko made a robot wave with her arm. "I love it. Looks

just like me."

"Thanks." Shelly smiled and snapped her sketchbook shut.

"Have you decided on a name yet?" Shelly asked Jules.

But Jules didn't answer. She had been unusually quiet as she scrolled through her phone.

"Hello . . . Jules?" Tomoko asked.

"One sec," Jules mumbled. She held her screen close, reading line after line.

"Oh. My. Gosh."

Jules waved her phone in the air. "You're never going to believe this!"

"Believe what?" Kenzie asked.

But Jules only jumped and waved her phone around until Kenzie snatched it out of her hand so the whole group could see. The screen showed the Austin roller derby league website. On the homepage was a colorful poster of two derby players going head-to-head.

Shelly squinted at the image. "There's an adult bout coming up?"

"Nope," Jules said. She zoomed into the part of the poster with all the information.

The Daredevils crowded together to read.

TX vs. NM Junior League Tournament

Refreshments! Games! Prizes!

One player named Star Skater

Saturday. Doors Open 1:30 p.m. First bout 2 p.m.

Tickets $12. Kids under 8, free.

"They're charging admission?" Tomoko's jaw hung open.

Jules clapped and nodded. "It's the big time! We're going to be real derby players!"

Kenzie's eyes gleamed as she handed Jules's phone back. "I wish Bree were here."

"I'll bet," Tomoko said, smiling.

Kenzie's cheeks turned pink. Everyone knew she had a crush on Bree.

Shelly threw her arm around Kenzie. "I wish she went here too," Shelly said. "But we'll see her today at the park. She's going to flip!"

"Yeah," Kenzie said wistfully. She leaned into Shelly.

The Daredevils all bumped fists and headed out to class. When they saw one another later at lunch, and again at recess, they talked about the tournament. Kenzie wondered if they'd get to keep any of the money from admission. Tomoko wondered if the prizes were for the skaters or the audience. Jules wanted to know if skaters would get free snacks at the snack bar.

Shelly wondered about all those things too. Or at least, she would have wondered about them if she weren't so focused on the one line of the poster everyone else seemed to miss.

The line made Shelly's seed of an idea bloom and stretch open. Her eyes got sparkly just thinking about it. Winning Star Skater was the *perfect* way to prove how important she was to the Daredevils! Then Shelly would have a special role like everyone else. Maybe she would even earn her dad's nickname, Shiny!

She just had to shine on the track enough to win.

CHAPTER FIVE

SHELLY HAD FIRE ON HER HEELS AS SHE ZOOMED OUT of school after the last bell.

"Wait!" Kenzie called.

Kenzie, Tomoko, and Jules stood at the top of the steps. Shelly paused at the sidewalk and looked over her shoulder.

"Race me!" Shelly said.

Tomoko and Jules kept walking normally, but Kenzie broke out and sprinted until she was at Shelly's side.

"How far?" Kenzie asked.

"To the park!" Shelly said. "And no hot lava game. Just racing."

Kenzie's eyebrows went up. Every time the girls raced, it was more like a make-believe adventure than running. But secretly, Shelly was already getting her plan started. If she practiced her speed off the track, it might help her win Star Skater at the tournament.

"And—go!"

Shelly and Kenzie puffed out their cheeks. They pumped their arms hard. Shelly's chest burned from running so fast. She zipped past all the usual Daredevils stops: the pizza place, the taco stand, the home of the Sour Birthday ice pop. All the shapes she usually stared at during their walk from school looked like a blurred watercolor painting.

Suddenly the grassy hills and tall park trees came into view. Shelly lowered her head. She ran faster than she had ever run before. She wondered if her legs looked more like wheels, the way they did on cartoon characters.

Shelly slapped her hand on their meeting rock.

"Made it! I win!"

Kenzie arrived a few seconds later.

"Jeez Louise," Kenzie panted. "When the heck did you get so fast?"

Shelly tried to answer, but she ended up coughing and laughing. Kenzie started laughing too. The girls sat in the shade and pulled their water bottles from their backpacks. They sipped on water and waited for Tomoko and Jules.

"What was that all about?" Tomoko asked.

"Speed work!" Shelly said.

"Speaking of speed . . ." Kenzie pointed toward the sidewalk, where Bree rumbled toward them on her skateboard.

"Ahoy!" Bree said. She pinned her hands to her hips and looked to the side, like the captain of a ship. The Daredevils laughed as Bree held her pose until her skateboard reached the rock. Bree kickflipped off her board and joined the others.

"What's new?" she asked.

Jules smiled mischievously. "Funny you should ask . . ."

She pulled out her phone and handed it to Bree. Kenzie leaned against Bree and clicked on the announcement.

"Oh *yes*," Bree said. "This poster is awesome. Do you think we'll get to play against the Cherry Pits too?"

"Shoot," Shelly said.

The others paused and looked at her.

Kenzie cocked her head. "What?"

"Oh." Shelly's cheeks went pink. She thought about Molly on the Cherry Pits, who practically barreled over the Daredevils at tryouts. That was exactly the kind of person who would get Star Skater. "I just . . . forgot they'd be playing."

Bree laughed. "They better," she said. "I'm ready for another race with their jammer." She leaped from the rock and stood in front of the others.

"Let's get in some *speeeeeed* practice," Bree yelled. Her voice went up and down, sounding exactly like a game show announcer.

Jules hopped off the rock and did a cartwheel over the grass. "Off-skates workout time!"

Shelly smiled and jumped down next to Jules. Kenzie and Tomoko stepped down after. The girls put their hands into a circle. Bree led their team chant.

"What are we?" she asked.

"Dare—" Tomoko and Kenzie said.

"Devils!" Shelly and Jules shouted.

"Dare—"

"Devils!"

"Dare—"

"Devils!"

All five girls yelled at once.

"Daredevils!"

Bree cupped her hands around her mouth. "Laps!"

"Come on," Kenzie said. "Laps? Like in PE?"

"Hey, don't knock PE," Bree said. She took off running toward the playground.

Shelly did her best to stay close at Bree's side, but the farther the team ran around the park, the harder it was to stay all together. The Daredevils started out running like an angry cluster of bees, but ended like a lazy kite tail flapping in the wind. Bree was first, then Shelly, then Kenzie, then Tomoko, and Jules last. They clutched their knees back at the rock, waiting for their breath to catch up.

"Rats," Shelly said. "You beat me."

Bree shook her head and grabbed her water. "Wasn't a race," she said. She set her bottle back down and reached for a stack of neon-green cones next to her bag.

"Zigzags!" Bree yelled.

The Daredevils set up the cones all around the field. Each cone was a few feet apart. Bree led the team in a line snaking their way through. When they made it one way, they changed order and snaked through again, and again.

Shelly was starting to have fun with the obstacle course. She even let her arms spin at her sides and ran like a giant windmill! She hopped from foot to foot.

"Woooo!" Shelly said.

Thwack.

Her calf smacked against one of the cones.

"Careful with those turns!" Bree called from the end of the line.

"She's working on her bruise collection!" Jules yelled.

Shelly rubbed her leg and kept jogging. "Right," she said. But Shelly doubted that Star Skater would be awarded to the kid with the most bruises.

Once the zigzags were done, Bree showed the team how to set up the course for their last drill: jammer jumps.

Everyone chucked their backpacks into one huge pile in the middle of the field. The players had to run to the pile, leap over it, then catch their balance and keep running on the other side. Bree went first so the others could see how to keep their feet together. The tower of backpacks went all the way to Bree's knees! Shelly wished she had the bouncy skates from her drawing.

"Hi-yah!" Jules said as she threw a kick in the air. She vaulted over the backpack stack and did a somersault in the grass.

"Nice one!" Tomoko called.

"Don't do that in skates, though," Kenzie added. "Or it will add some major bruises to your collection."

Jules laughed and brushed the grass from her arms.

Shelly was the last one to go. Bree, Kenzie, Tomoko, and Jules cheered from the other side.

"Let's go, Bomb Shell!" Bree called. "Show those backpacks who's boss!"

Shelly took a deep breath. She crouched in her classic derby stance, then jolted forward, racing across the field.

"Yeah Shelly!" the others said. The tower of backpacks loomed in front of her. Shelly pulled her legs up and—

Oof.

Shelly landed right on top of the pile. Bree ran over.

"That was great!" she said. "You kept your feet together and everything! You just caught one of the straps coming down."

Shelly pulled her legs in and wrapped her arms around them. Her plan for winning Star Skater wasn't exactly getting off to a great start.

Kenzie, Tomoko, and Jules sat down beside Bree.

"Who's leading tomorrow?" Kenzie asked.

Shelly looked at the others nervously, waiting for someone else to volunteer. She still had no idea what kind of practice she could lead.

"I will!" Jules said. "I'll call it 'Collecting Bruises 101.'" She grinned and pulled her phone out of her bag.

"Or maybe just 'Hip Checking 101,'" Kenzie said.

Jules sighed. "Yeah, yeah . . . Hey! The tournament poster has a link to the New Mexico teams!"

The Daredevils huddled around the screen.

"Check out that one team!" Tomoko said. She pointed to a group of girls dressed in pink shirts. "They have horns on their helmets! Like unicorns!"

"Ha, that's awesome!" Bree said.

Shelly leaned forward. There was something about the picture that made a little firefly in her head flicker and sputter to life. She never knew teams could put horns on their helmets.

She studied the line of skaters and smiled. They looked like they had come right out of her sketchbook.

CHAPTER SIX

TUESDAYS WERE THE ART ROTATION AT SCHOOL, WHICH meant it was the one day of the week Shelly got to set her sketchbook out on her desk instead of hiding it over her lap.

"Squiggles!" the art teacher announced.

"Yes!" Shelly whispered. She loved squiggle exercises. Shelly positioned her pencil over the blank page as the teacher took a piece of yellow chalk and made a tiny point on the blackboard. The chalk twisted around and around.

"There," the teacher said. She turned again to the class. "Copy the shape and turn it into anything from your imagination!"

The way squiggles worked was that the teacher first made a weird half-drawing, then the students had to fit it into a picture somehow. Shelly had made zigzags into light-ning bolts and swirls into water. She had made a wiggly line into a person dancing and a bunch of little curlicues into a bowl of worms.

She got to work, extending the half circles on the board into wheels of roller skates zooming over the track. She filled the skates with feet and legs and the full body of Ken-zilla, roaring and swiping through the air. This time, Shelly gave Kenzilla gloves that turned into claws at the end. She finished the last claw tip and smiled. Her picture reminded her of the unicorn helmets she had seen the day before.

Shelly wouldn't have minded wearing claws herself at Jules's "Bruises 101" practice that after-noon.

"Through the tunnel again!" Jules cried. Shelly huffed and barreled forward across the field. She wore one backpack on her front and another on her back. According to Jules, the bags were sup-posed to be protection. Instead, they just felt like bulky weight sagging Shelly's shoulders down.

The four other girls stood in two lines of two, with a narrow tunnel between them. As Shelly ran into the tunnel, everyone threw their hips into Shelly's side. Shelly dug her feet into the ground to keep her balance, but she couldn't help getting jostled back and forth.

"Nice, Bomb Shell! You made it!" Jules called once Shelly was through.

"Wearing shoes," Shelly said. She shrugged off the bags and let them fall with a heavy thud on the grass. "In skates I would have wiped out!"

Tomoko lifted one bag onto her back, then reached for the other.

"I think the point is to be ready to wipe out," Tomoko said. "Most skaters can't stay on their feet all the time."

"Yeah . . ." Shelly said. But with the tournament coming up, she didn't want to be like *most* skaters. She wanted to be a *Star Skater*.

Tomoko finished her turn and volunteered to lead the next day just as Shelly's mom came down the sidewalk. Shelly waved to the others and grabbed her bag. After wearing two bags on her shoulders, her one backpack seemed a lot lighter than usual. Or maybe Shelly was getting stronger.

Shelly's mom hugged Shelly close to her side. She ran her hand through Shelly's hair.

"Missed you," she said.

Shelly smelled the clay on her mom's dress. She smiled. "Missed you too."

They crossed the field to the back lot where Shelly's mom had parked the old VW van. On Sundays, Shelly's mom liked the long walk to her art class. On Tuesdays, she traded the long walk for a short drive.

The VW rumbled down South Congress, across Lady Bird Lake, and over to East Austin. Almost every building had colorful murals painted along the side. There were aliens and movie stars and even giant breakfast foods dancing the cha-cha. The van dipped into a small parking lot nestled between a car wash and a veterinary hospital. The studio above the vet was part of a community art space where her mom taught.

The stairwell door opened into a large room with easels and desks scattered everywhere.

"Good evening," Shelly's mom said. She hung her sweater on a hook by the door. "I've brought the mini artist with me."

Heads popped out from behind their easels one by one. An older woman with short, blue-tinted hair peered over her glasses. Her mouth made an O of pleasant surprise.

"Shelly!" Mrs. Otterloo said. "I have some extra candies in my bag."

Shelly smiled.

Fen, another art student and one of Shelly's friends in the class, waved from one corner of the room.

"Observing or participating today?" they asked. They held a charcoal stick out toward Shelly, inviting her in.

Shelly's mom looked at Shelly and raised her eyebrows.

Shelly glanced at the charcoal and back at her mom. "Um, participating," she said. She sat down at the station next to Fen.

"What are you making today?" Shelly asked.

Fen scratched their square jaw and stared at the easel in front of them thoughtfully. "Don't know yet." They looked at Shelly and smiled. "Inspiration can come from anywhere, anytime!"

"Yeah," Shelly said, though she wasn't exactly sure if inspiration would hit her tonight. Unlike with the squiggle exercises, students were allowed to draw anything they wanted in her mom's art class. It didn't have to start with a weird half-shape. The only catch was that once the students finished drawing, they had to form a hunk of clay into a 3-D version of their picture.

Shelly had watched her mom's class tons of times. She could move things from her head to paper, but moving a picture to a real thing seemed impossible. She glanced at the block of clay in front of her. It didn't seem like it wanted to be anything else except clay.

She shook her head. No wonder they called it a "block" when you couldn't think of what to do.

Scritch-scritch, scritch-scritch.

The sound of charcoal over paper echoed around the room. But Shelly's easel was still blank. She reached into her backpack and pulled out her sketchbook.

"That looks interesting." Fen gazed at the picture Shelly had drawn of Kenzie with the claws.

Shelly blushed. "I made it today."

Fen nodded at the clay next to Shelly. "Bring it to life!"

Shelly blinked and looked down at her sketchbook. "I can't make a person."

"Oh," Fen said. They tapped at Kenzie's pointy fingertips. "I meant the glove design."

Glove design?

Fen's words bounced around in Shelly's head. They got bigger and bigger with every breath, like a party balloon filling up with air.

Shelly thought about the photo of the New Mexico team with the unicorn helmets. She thought about her sketches of bouncy skates and derby jerseys with wings.

Roller derby was about being strong and brave . . . but it was also about being creative and different. Mambo had told the group to work on their team strategy *and* their look. Maybe that meant Star Skater wasn't just about skating fast. Maybe the title could go to someone with the most awesome new derby gear!

Shelly's eyes gleamed as she imagined her pictures coming to life.

Instead of doing silly sketches that made her teammates laugh, Shelly could turn her drawings into real *designs* that would make the Daredevils the coolest things on wheels!

But Shelly's gear wouldn't just look good. It would help the team skate faster, and block better . . . all the things Shelly needed help with on the track. She imagined gear that would let her do quadruple spins and high jumps. That would have to get her named as Star Skater!

Shelly pulled the block of clay in front of her. She dipped her hands into a bowl of water, then got to work ripping a piece off the side.

At the end of class, the students all got up and wandered around the room to look at one another's creations. Some people made figurines. Some had shaped the clay into other materials, camouflaging it as driftwood or stones.

Fen made a miniature version of a tall building downtown that Shelly called the "owl building." Fen told her the real name was the Frost Bank Tower, but smiled and said that "owl building" was better. Mrs. Otterloo made a pear-shaped birdhouse, which she quickly informed everyone was actually a house for her two pet tarantulas, Minnie and Ginny.

Everyone gathered around Shelly's station last.

"How lovely," Mrs. Otterloo cooed. "What is it?"

"It's a claw," Shelly said. "Well, actually it's a roller derby glove that looks like a claw. I designed it."

The others nodded thoughtfully. Shelly felt like a real artist, standing there in front of her work. She couldn't wait to surprise the Daredevils with her super-amazing plan.

CHAPTER SEVEN

SHELLY'S SKETCHBOOK WAS FILLING UP FAST WITH ideas for winning Star Skater. She had to remind herself to look up from the pages in class or when shoveling food into her mouth at lunch. Derby practices were the hardest, since she had to put her sketchbook away completely.

Tomoko brought everyone onto the park field Wednesday afternoon. Instead of forming a tunnel like they did in hip-checking practice or a line like in Bree's practice, Tomoko had the team pretend they were on the derby track. She clustered the blockers close together.

"Now we're going to jog slowly—"

"Jogging?" Jules said. "I thought we already did jogging!"

"That was speed work!" Bree called from behind. "We didn't jog, we flew!"

Bree stood half a field away, raring to come crashing into the group.

The blockers started lumbering forward. Tomoko turned to Jules. "We're not working on speed," she said. "Bree gets to run, but we don't. She has the speed advantage, just like jammers in real bouts. We have to practice our form for when Bree gets to us."

When the Daredevils scrimmaged against other teams on the league, Shelly and the blockers didn't block Bree—they helped her find an opening, and they blocked the opposite jammer. But in practice, Bree had to switch back and forth between being herself and the opposing team's jammer. Right now, she was pretending to be on the other team.

"Here I come!" Bree yelled. She took off sprinting across the field.

The blockers checked for Bree over their shoulders.

"Labyrinth!" Tomoko said. Labyrinth was a blocking plan Tomoko and Kenzie came up with the week before. The blocking pack split into two pairs: Shelly and Kenzie, then Tomoko and Jules. When Bree made it to one pair, the other raced ahead. That way, if Bree passed one set of blockers, there was always another set ahead of her.

"Like a never-ending labyrinth," Kenzie explained.

Shelly felt a jolt on her left hip. Bree's momentum had split the Dynamic Duo in two.

"Next level!" Shelly called.

Tomoko and Jules scrambled ahead. Bree spun and dove and squirmed between them.

Jules waved her arm. "Next level!"

The team went like that for the rest of the lap around the field, racing ahead and throwing walls in front of Bree. But Bree broke through every time.

"I'm not good at this," Shelly said as Bree slid past her.

Tomoko whistled and the group slowed down. They walked back to their meeting rock.

"Yes you are," Kenzie said. "Bree's just an awesome jammer. She makes it look easy."

Bree smiled and elbowed Kenzie's arm.

"Are you kidding? That blocking play is SO good. I could get through two of you at a time, but not all four! And Jules, those hip checks were killing me!"

The Daredevils spread out over the grass. They stretched their hands and feet like they were making snow angels. Kenzie studied the sky overhead.

"See any shapes in the clouds?" Tomoko asked.

Kenzie smiled. "I see us looking awesome at the tournament!"

Shelly squeezed a clump of grass. Her hands felt itchy without a pencil.

Zip!

Shelly pulled out her sketchbook. She leaned against the rock and thought about the Labyrinth move again. Maybe there was a way to keep the jammer behind them longer, without having to race ahead over and over. Something to help the blockers stay squeezed together.

She turned to the page with the Kenzilla claws. If Shelly

put something sticky on the palms and fingers, Kenzie could stick tight to Shelly whenever they formed a blocker wall. Then the jammer could never get through! Shelly got to work adding sticky dots to her design.

"Another picture?"

Shelly felt a little tap on her elbow. She clutched the drawing tight to her chest.

"Whoa." Kenzie bounced back on her heels. She looked hurt. "You always show your drawings."

"Yeah," Shelly said slowly. Her hands relaxed a little. "But this isn't just a drawing for fun. It's for the tournament."

"Are you leading practice tomorrow?" Kenzie asked.

Shelly shook her head. She needed more time to pull her plan together. "Friday," she said. "When we meet behind the warehouse. I have a plan. You'll see."

The other Daredevils were all looking at Shelly. Bree had an eyebrow raised.

"You don't usually keep secrets," Tomoko said.

Shelly paused. Was she keeping a secret? If she was, it didn't feel like the bad kind of secret. It felt like a good secret, the kind that buzzed through her bones and made her warm just by holding it safe inside her.

"It's not really a secret," Shelly said. "It's more of a . . . sur-prise!" She squeezed her mouth shut tight before she could say too much. The excitement moved up into her cheeks. It spread down to her toes and made them tap and wiggle.

"Ooh, I love surprises!" Jules said.

Kenzie smiled. "Me too."

The warm feeling inside Shelly's chest thrummed.

"Speaking of surprises . . ." Jules jumped on top of their rock, casting a shadow over the grass.

"What?" Bree asked.

"I have a derby name," Jules announced.

Everyone shifted to look at Jules. Shelly flipped to a blank page in her notebook. Her pencil was at the ready.

Jules clutched at the air and slowly folded her arms in front of her.

"What are you doing?" Kenzie said.

Jules narrowed her eyes. "It's called *pantomime*. We used to do it all the time in drama club. I'm *pant-o-miming* an invisible cloak."

Shelly found a line in her head like the squiggle on her art teacher's chalkboard. She let her pencil make the swoosh of a cloak blowing in the wind. She looked back up at Jules, who had frozen into a statue.

"Well?" Tomoko said. "Tell us!"

Jules suddenly tossed the invisible cloak behind her shoulder and raised her chin in the air.

"You may call me," she said in a fake British accent, "Crown Jules."

"Sweet!" Bree said. "All hail Crown Jules!"

The girls stretched their hands to the sky.

"All hail Crown Jules!"

Jules laughed and jumped back into the grass.

"Smooth," Tomoko said. "Super regal."

Shelly didn't hear anything after that. The page in front of her stretched on and on until it filled up her whole world. She drew Jules posed on the derby track the same way she had posed on the rock. Shelly shaped Jules's helmet into a crown. Over her derby gear, Shelly made a thick, fuzzy cloak that flew out behind Jules when she skated.

Bruise prevention technology! Shelly wrote under the cloak. That was something else she could design!

BRUISE PREVENTION TECHNOLOGY!

"Did you make a drawing for Jules?"

Shelly's paper world curled in at the edges. She peeked over her sketchbook and saw Kenzie in front of her.

"I'll show you later," Shelly said. She bumped Kenzie's fist. "On Friday."

Kenzie did the Dynamic Duo handshake with Shelly, though she made a face like she had been hip checked in the gut. Shelly frowned and turned back to her drawing. She wasn't shutting the others out, she told herself. She was getting the surprise ready. Plus, Shelly didn't need the other Daredevils poking holes in her ideas before she even finished. She had to see her designs through.

She had to get Star Skater.

CHAPTER EIGHT

SHELLY STUDIED HER LIST AGAIN.

Kenzilla claws—extra sticky handholds

Crown Jules cloak—to cushion bad falls

Tomonater glasses—for spotting jammers

Bomb Shell . . .

She bit the end of her eraser. What could she do for her own derby name?

Maybe an exploding wrist guard? She could hide confetti packets in little pouches, then release them right when the other team's jammer came around. She and Kenzie could even make a special game play out of it!

Shelly started to draw herself on the page before she remembered that she wasn't really good at self-portraits. What did her nose look like again? Shelly picked up the

spoon from her cereal bowl and faced it away. She stared at
her reflection in the silver.

"My face looks weird," Shelly said.

Her mom laughed. "Everyone's face looks weird in a
spoon. Want me to grab a hand mirror?"

"No thanks," Shelly said. She moved her pencil over the
page quickly, making a squiggle that turned into a wrist
guard with confetti exploding out of one end. That was all
she really needed for her derby gear project.

Shelly's mom set her cup of tea down over the newspaper. "I should have your Kenzilla claw back from the kiln
by tonight. Is it a gift for Kenzie?"

Shelly's pencil froze. "No," she said.

Her mom seemed surprised. "Oh?"

"It's a model," Shelly said. "I'm designing derby gear for the team. That's my job for the tournament."

"Your . . . job?" her mom asked.

Shelly nodded. "Everyone has a job. Bree's is to be fast and Jules taught us about bruises and Tomoko knows how to block and Kenzie's in charge of the plays."

Her mom picked up her mug. "I thought you did all those things too."

Shelly turned back to her drawing. "I do," she said. She used her careful, explaining voice. "But I'm not the best at them. I'm the best at derby gear designs, so it's my job."

Shelly's mom slurped her tea down. "Hmmm." At first Shelly thought the sound was just how good the tea was. Then her mom cleared her throat. "You know, whenever I work on an art collaboration with someone, we don't each do one job."

Shelly glanced up.

"The other artist and I, we work together. We plan things out together and sketch together and then sculpt side by side. That way the art feels whole to both of us. Not something we each gave half to. Do you know what I mean?"

Shelly smooshed her mouth together. She was trying to decide whether or not she knew what her mom meant. One whole thing was a lot better than two halves. By the time Shelly showed her designs to the Daredevils, she wanted them to see the whole idea, not a bunch of half ideas. That was why she had to finish everything on her own.

"Yeah," Shelly said. "I know what you mean."

Her mom smiled.

Shelly's phone buzzed. A text from Kenzie hovered over the screen.

Pre-practice meeting before school.

"Got to go! Daredevils morning bathroom meeting in thirty minutes!"

"Can't miss that," her mom said. She shooed Shelly up from the table. "See you after derby practice."

Shelly flung her backpack on, kissed her mom, and left her house in a hurry. But she had only taken a few steps before she forgot about running late to the meeting.

As Shelly turned out of her driveway, two skateboarders zipped past on either side of the sidewalk. Shelly jumped out of the way, her heart racing.

"Hey!" Shelly said. She hated it when other kids got so close to her like that. It was like they were trying to scare her.

Then Shelly remembered what had happened at the Free Skate night last Saturday, when the kids on in-line skates made her lose her balance. Shelly pulled out her sketchbook and started brainstorming.

"Balance," Shelly murmured. "How to keep balance . . ."

She drew an acrobat holding a stick over a tight rope. A stick would get in the way on the track. She looked ahead at the boys. It took balance to stay on a skateboard. Shelly drew a figure leaning forward. When she tried to balance, she usually made her feet go wide. Was there a way to do that on skates? Another balloon idea suddenly inflated in her head.

Bubble boots!

Shelly drew a derby player with big, wide skates. No one could get knocked over in those! She stomped her feet as she walked, making long, clomping steps as she pretended to wear bubble boots until she got to school. By the time Shelly nudged the bathroom door open, the Daredevils glowered at her like she was a plate of mystery meat.

"Where have you been?" Kenzie asked. "I'm telling everyone the plan for practice today."

"Sorry," Shelly said. She shook the invisible boots off her feet.

At some point, Shelly definitely wrote down the notes for Kenzie's practice. She must have—she always took notes at derby planning meetings. Plus, in the bathroom Kenzie had said something about specific code words, and hand motions the players had to remember, which was exactly the kind of thing that went into Shelly's notes.

But as Shelly flipped through her sketchbook at lunch, and later on after class, she couldn't find anything about Kenzie's game plays. Instead, the pages were overflowing with Shelly's designs. She had drawn the bubble boots over and over, changing little details each time, trying to get them exactly right. She drew Kenzie's gloves again, along with Tomoko's glasses and Jules's cloak and her own exploding confetti wrist guard.

Shelly wondered what she could design for Bree. Probably something that had to do with being fast.

What could help a jammer . . . Shelly wondered.

"Watch it!"

Shelly jumped back as someone dipped out of the school auditorium. They were carrying a huge stack of folded bed-sheets that towered above their head. The top few sheets swayed back and forth.

"Sorry," Shelly said. She gazed up at the tower, following each fold down until she saw Camila's face poking out from the side. "What are you doing with all those sheets?"

"They're not sheets," Camila said. "They're costumes. Drama club is putting on a performance in three weeks! I barely have time to put everything together!"

"Three weeks sounds like a long time," Shelly said. She glanced at her list. "I have to make a bunch of stuff in just one day."

Camila's eyebrows went up. "For what?"

"The derby team," Shelly said. She flinched a moment, worried that Camila would be mad she was talking about roller derby. Camila had nearly joined the Daredevils' team earlier in the season, up until she put on skates and realized she hated skating.

But Camila didn't seem mad. She seemed interested. "What kind of stuff?"

Shelly turned her head one way, then the other. The halls were slowly emptying as kids slammed their lockers shut and ran for the doors to go home. The rest of the

Daredevils were probably outside on the steps. And since Camila wasn't technically on the team anymore, that meant she could see the surprise *before* it was ready.

"I'm designing things for the team to wear," Shelly said. She rotated her sketchbook and showed Camila her pictures.

"Awesome!" Camila said. "You're doing costumes too!"

Shelly frowned. "No, I'm not. This is special derby gear."

Camila shrugged. "OK," she said. "I was just going to offer some help." She nodded to a door farther down the hall that said BACKSTAGE. "Could you get that for me?"

"Sure," Shelly said. She grabbed the handle. Camila shuffled through the doorway, keeping her tower of costumes steady.

Shelly was about to let the door close. Then she stuck her head down the darkened hall after Camila. "Help with what?"

Camila looked over her shoulder and smiled.

"Come to the crypt and see."

CHAPTER NINE

CRYPT?

Shelly's eyes nearly popped out of her head. "You mean like a grave or something?"

Camila stopped backstage.

"Of course not," she said. "The crypt is what we call the costume room. It's in the basement. Come on."

Shelly was still holding the door open. She glanced toward the front of the school. Today was Kenzie's practice out at the park. But Shelly still couldn't find the game play notes. Would it be better to miss and have her surprise ready for tomorrow, or not be ready for either day?

"Wait up!" Shelly called.

She crept into the darkened hall and pulled up the Dynamic Duo message thread on her phone.

Gotta stay after school, Shelly texted Kenzie.

What about practice?

Shelly bit her lip.

Tomorrow, she wrote. Sorry!

Shelly turned her phone around and used her screen as a flashlight.

"Why is it so dark in here?" Shelly asked.

"They're figuring out how they want to light the stage," Camila said, "so the other lights have to stay off." She stopped in front of a metal gate and nodded at the latch.

Shelly swung the gate open. As Camila passed by, Shelly reached up and took the top half of Camila's stack.

"Thanks," Camila said. Her nose peeked over the material. "Now I can see!"

They went down a set of metal stairs. Shelly blinked, her eyes adjusting to the darkness. Camila set her things down on a bench and flipped a switch by the bottom step.

"Whoa."

Warm light filled the room, which Shelly could now see was crammed from corner to corner with racks of clothes. Shelly set her pile next to Camila's. She wandered through the crypt, touching the clothes as she passed. There were thick, fuzzy coats perfect for Jules's cloak, and scaly pleather jackets for Kenzie's gloves.

"This is great," Shelly said.

"Check out the accessory wall," Camila said, hitching her thumb. Behind her were huge plastic tubs stacked one on top of the other. Each had a label like SCARVES & HAND-KERCHIEFS or GLASSES.

Shelly pointed to the one marked GLASSES. "Can I look in there? I'm making a pair of red laser glasses."

Camila shook her head. "All the stuff on hangers and in tubs have to stay here," she said. She pointed to the far corner of the room. "But that's all free for taking."

"Hmmm." Shelly stepped toward the corner, where a giant heap of costumes and accessories were squeezed together like a block of mishmashed clay. Would she be able to see something in the block this time?

She took out her sketchbook and flipped through her pictures, trying to figure out how to match the things in front of her with the sketches on the page.

Shelly reached into the corner and fished out a pair of plain black gloves. The Kenzilla claws in Shelly's sketchbook had lizard skin and pointy fingertips. Still, the important part of Shelly's design was to help handholds in blocking moves. If Shelly found a bunch of sticky dots and put them on the fingers and palm, plain gloves could do the job.

"Check this out," Camila said. She kneeled into the pile, pulling out a green leotard covered in sequins.

"Very . . . sparkly," Shelly said. She turned back to the gloves.

"It's ripped at the side," Camila said, frowning. Her face brightened. "But look! There's more!" She fished out another leotard covered in purple sequins, then one in blue, another in red, and a fifth in yellow.

"A whole set! And you could cut out parts of them!"

Shelly squinted at the glittering rainbow. "I guess that could look cool," she said. She thought about the rest of her derby gear designs. "But they don't *do* anything."

Camila shrugged. She left the leotards bunched up together and went back to the costumes on the bench. "I have to work on this," she said. "You OK over there?"

Shelly nodded. "Thanks again," she said. "This will be great."

Under the gentle buzzing of the crypt lights, Shelly sifted through the pile. She pulled out a giant roll of bubble wrap. She found a scuffed foam head to carve up for Bree's gear. She found an old fuzzy blanket that could be a queen's cloak if it really wanted to. She even found a pair of fake glasses for the Tomonater.

"Perfect!" Shelly said. She placed the glasses along with the other things into a giant paper bag Camila found. Camila tucked the sequined leotards at the bottom.

"Just in case," she said.

Shelly hoisted the bag up. Now she was the one lumbering under a huge mass of clothes. Camila held the metal gate open. "You got it?"

"I got it," Shelly said. She gave an awkward wave and stumbled down the hall.

The light outside felt a million times brighter after being down in the crypt with Camila. Shelly dragged the giant paper bag behind her as she turned onto the main street. The shops buzzed with people.

Now that Austin was slipping deeper into April, the early summer air swept into the city. Shelly passed teenagers wearing dresses with cowboy boots, tie-dye shorts with denim jackets, and long-sleeved sheer blouses cinched at the waist. She even walked by a woman emerging out of a store wearing a turquoise-sequined dress. Shelly thought about the leotards Camila had stuffed in her bag. But she had to stay focused on designing the gear in her notebook. Sequins weren't going to earn her Star Skater.

Shelly turned into a store with a sign that said ROUGH DRAFT CRAFTS overhead. She left her bag by the checkout counter and got to work collecting bottles of glue, a set of fabric paint, a paintbrush, sticky strips, confetti, duct tape, and anything else that could be useful for making the things on her list.

She set the bundle next to the cash register, then craned her neck around the store.

"Uh, hello?" Shelly asked.

"Hi!"

Someone popped up on the other side of the counter. "Sorry, there's a wobbly leg under here." It was Fen! They blinked and shook their head. "Shelly! You're getting art supplies?"

"Sort of," Shelly said. "Derby supplies. My roller derby team is trying out new gear, like the claw I made from the clay."

"Neat," Fen said. They rang Shelly up and added the glue and rolls of tape to her large paper bag.

Shelly tugged the bag behind her. "See you later," she said.

"Wait." Fen ducked under the counter again and

brought out a handful of paintbrushes. "These were left over from a craft night a while back. You'll need brushes for your teammates, right?"

Shelly stared at the brushes in Fen's hand. She wanted to have everything done before her turn at leading practice. But there wasn't enough time. Shelly thought about what her mom had said that morning about art collaboration. It was best to have things finished, and to finish her idea, Shelly needed the team.

"Thank you," Shelly said. She added the brushes to her bag.

"Teamwork makes the dream work!" Fen said cheerfully. They dipped back under the counter to continue fixing the wobbly leg.

Shelly left the shop and walked to meet her mom by the edge of the park.

The practice field was on the other side of the block, but Shelly thought she could see the Daredevils past the playground equipment, running and jumping back and forth. It was weird to not be with her teammates. She wondered how drills were going with one less person on the field. Were they having a hard time without her?

She paused. What if practice was going even better without Shelly there?

Shelly squeezed the handles of her bag. She had a solid plan to show the team how important she was. They'd see her awesome drawings, then help put the gear together and take over the track! She took out her sketchbook and jotted down an agenda for tomorrow's practice.

Show the designs.
Make the gear.
Practice for the tournament.

She hugged her notebook to her chest and mustered a smile. Soon the others would see that Shelly had a special place on the team too.

CHAPTER TEN

THE AIR FELT CHILLY THE MOMENT SHELLY STEPPED inside the hall at school the next morning. Shelly wasn't sure why exactly until she turned the corner and saw Kenzie standing next to the bathroom door.

"Hey Kenzilla."

Shelly had stuck her hand out for a Dynamic Duo handshake, but Kenzie didn't unfold her arms. She didn't say hello back, or bump fists, or pretend to spit over her shoulder. At lunch, the Daredevils sat across from one another, staring into space and chewing on tater tots.

"Wanna swing?" Shelly asked at recess. Kenzie only shrugged and let Shelly drag her by the sleeve.

The swing set creaked as Shelly and Kenzie swayed next to each other.

"So . . . how was practice?" Shelly asked.

Kenzie grunted.

"Did you work on the plays?"

Kenzie dug her shoe into the playground sand. "You would know if you came," she muttered.

Shelly squeezed the chains on either side of her swing. "Yeah," she said. "I really wanted to. I just had to get things ready for my practice."

"How come your practice is more important?" Kenzie asked. She looked at Shelly. Shelly felt a weird mix of guilt and something else. *Was* her practice more important than

Kenzie's? Did that mean Shelly was starting to be more important too?

"I needed supplies," Shelly said. "We're going to make stuff."

Kenzie raised an eyebrow. "Like what?"

"You'll see," Shelly said. She smiled. "It's really cool, though. It will help us skate better." She held a fist out to Kenzie. "I'll be there for you next time. I promise. Dynamic Duo?"

Her hand hovered for a moment.

"You really promise?" Kenzie asked.

"Cross my laces," Shelly said.

Kenzie sighed, then tapped her knuckles to Shelly.

"OK. Dynamic Duo."

Shelly, Kenzie, Tomoko, and Jules decided to play the game "switch off" on the way to the warehouse. When it was one girl's turn, the others would call out how she had to walk. Tomoko had to shuffle backward. Kenzie did a pretend hopscotch. Jules had to spin every five steps. Shelly took each step at a different height.

"Now on tiptoe! Now lunge! Now regular! Squat down! Back on tiptoe! Limbo!"

Jules called out each step to Shelly. Shelly raised her feet like a ballerina. She squatted and leaped like a frog. She shimmied under an invisible limbo pole.

"Crawl like a baby!" Jules called.

"Gross. I'm not touching the sidewalk with my hands," Shelly said.

Jules held her chin. "Hmm, OK. Then duck down like a branch is going to smack you in the face."

Shelly hunched over and took a step.

"What are you doing?" Bree asked. She met the girls at the corner.

Jules threw her arms out. "Pre-practice warm up!"

Bree pointed at her chest. "My turn, then."

"Lava round!" Shelly said. "Stay off the sidewalk. Anything else is safe."

"Got it," Bree said. She jumped in the air and landed on a sewer grate. The others watched as Bree bounded from the grate to a stoplight pole to a rug in front of one of the shops.

"You look like a grasshopper," Kenzie said.

Bree laughed. She sprang from one spot to the next until they reached the warehouse.

"Guess we're warmed up," Tomoko said as the group walked inside.

The Daredevils got their skates and gear from the rental

counter. Shelly looked around the front entrance. She leaned across the counter and peered back where the skates were all lined up.

Pearl Jammer was behind the counter again.

"I already got your special skates," Pearl said. "Yellow spot and everything."

Shelly smiled. "Thanks. Did my mom drop off a big bag here earlier?"

"Hold on." She rolled behind the rows of skates and pulled out Shelly's bulky brown paper bag.

"So this is the surprise," Bree said.

Kenzie eyed the bag suspiciously, but took hold of one handle while Shelly grabbed another.

"Let's head over by the snack bar first," Shelly said. "We gotta make this stuff before we use it."

"Use what?" Tomoko asked.

They dumped their gear next to the bleachers and sat at one of the tables. The giant brown bag leaned against Shelly's side. She stood at the end of the table, the other Daredevils looking back at her, waiting.

This was her big chance.

Shelly fished out her notebook and cracked it open.

"Surprise!" she cried. "The drawings are coming to life!"

Kenzie laughed. "I'm turning into a lizard monster and stomping on people?"

"I'm pretty sure that's illegal," Tomoko said, chuckling. "Or at least against the rules."

Shelly squeezed her eyes shut. Was the team laughing at her?

"This is important," Shelly said. She didn't mean to yell it, but when she opened her eyes again the others were staring back at her. Shelly took a breath. "I designed new derby gear for the tournament."

"Like costumes?" Jules asked.

Shelly shook her head. "No, not like costumes. This is real gear, like skates and elbow pad–level gear. We're going to make it and then practice with it."

"Oh." Bree's eyes slid across the table and met with Kenzie's. Shelly pretended not to notice.

She brought out one thing after another from her bag. She piled the gloves in front of Kenzie. She set the glasses before Tomoko. She shoved the blanket over to Jules.

"And we're making a cone for the back of your helmet out of this," Shelly told Bree as she took out the foam head. "So you can go faster."

She brought out the glue and tape from Rough Draft Crafts, then kicked the bag toward the bleachers. The only things left inside were the old leotards Camila had packed in.

As Shelly turned back to the table, she realized no one had reached for anything.

"Why are we doing this?" Kenzie asked.

"We're adding to the basic gear so we can shine on the track," Shelly said. "Like that one team from New Mexico. They skate with unicorn helmets, right?"

"Well . . ." Tomoko tapped her fingers. "I think the horns are detachable once they hit the track, though. It's just for the look."

Shelly's eyes went wide. "Just for the look? Just for the *look*?" She held up a Kenzilla glove. "The right gear could make the difference between letting a jammer through. Or getting ahead of the other team. We have to make the *best* stuff so we can skate our best!"

Shelly banged her hand on the table. Jules jolted upright and made a salute.

"Yes, Captain!"

The others giggled.

"It's not funny!" Shelly said.

And something in her voice finally went all the way over, creeping up a hill of wanting to be important to the team, and suddenly tumbling down the other side where Shelly *needed* the others to take her seriously. Where it wasn't enough to have them laugh at her drawings anymore. She wanted the team to use her ideas for real.

Shelly pointed at Tomoko. "You're going to use the fabric

paint to make the glasses red," Shelly said. "And Kenzie, I need you to glue sticky dots on the gloves. Jules, you can cut the blanket into a cloak and then glue two corners together."

The team sat in silence. After a moment, Jules reached across the table and picked up a pair of scissors. Kenzie squeezed a dot of glue on one of the gloves. Bree sized up the foam head. Tomoko picked up a brush and tube of paint.

Shelly folded her arms and nodded.

"Teamwork makes the dream work," she said to herself.

CHAPTER ELEVEN

THE DAREDEVILS SAT AT THE TABLE, SNIPPING AND gluing and taping things together. They weren't really laughing and goofing around, which would have been really weird a couple weeks ago. But Shelly told herself it was fine. There wasn't a lot of time to goof around when making super-cool new derby gear.

She finished gluing a pouch of confetti to the inside of her wrist guard, then waved her arm in front of her.

"Bam!" Shelly said.

Nothing happened.

"Hmmm." Shelly took the scissors and cut a tiny hole into the top of the pouch so confetti could come out easier. She clapped her wrists together.

"Bomb Shell attack! Boom!"

In her head, the confetti was supposed to shoot out of the pouch in every direction. But in real life, Shelly just felt the pouch dig into her wrist. She growled and took the wrist guard off. There had to be something she could wear at the tournament. Shelly looked over her sketchbook. The bubble boots! She could make those. She grabbed the roll of bubble wrap.

Jules slathered half a bottle of glue over one corner of the blanket. She tossed a handful of Shelly's discarded confetti on. "You got a derby name yet, Bree?"

Bree shrugged. "Sort of, yeah."

The others paused and looked up at her.

"Well?" Tomoko asked.

"Well, at first I was thinking Beastly Bree. But that makes me sound like a werewolf or something. Then I was thinking Bree's Knees, like the bee's knees. But that's way too cutesy."

"You're so fast," Kenzie said. "Maybe your name can be, like, a speedy name."

"Exactly!" Bree pointed at Kenzie. "I'm fast. But I'm also smooth on the track. Here's what I came up with . . ."

Everyone leaned in. Even Shelly forgot about her gear for a moment.

"I'm going by Bree-Zee!" Bree said.

"Awesome!" Tomoko said.

Kenzie bumped fists with Bree.

"The Bree-Zee jammer." Jules made a frame around Bree's face. "She zips past blockers before they even see her coming! All they feel is a breeze."

"Yeah," Bree said, laughing.

Shelly's hands were on her sketchbook before she even realized. She started drawing a picture of Bree zooming across the page. She could wear sky-blue leggings and have propellers on the back of her skates and—

"What's that?"

Bree's finger landed on the helmet Shelly had drawn.

"It's the extra piece we're making," Shelly said. "I've seen it on cars. You'll end up going faster on the track if your helmet comes to a point at the end."

"Ummm . . ." Bree held up the chunk of foam in front of her. "No offense, Bomb Shell, but I'm not gluing this to my helmet."

Shelly dropped her pencil. "Why not?"

"A million reasons," Bree said. "Jammers have to wear covers on their helmets, the cone will probably fall off and trip someone else, and oh yeah, I don't want to glue anything to my head!"

Shelly was just about to respond when the front doors to the derby warehouse burst open. Shelly watched as two adult derby players waltzed inside. One of them was Wreck-the-Holls, from the Hazel Nuts team. Shelly usually called her Ms. E.

"Hey Mom," Kenzie said.

"Hey Daredevils!" Ms. E. waved and slung a pair of skates over her shoulder.

"We better go," Shelly said. "Looks like adult practice is starting."

She collected all the supplies—including Bree's helmet piece—back into her bag. The Daredevils then picked up their own pairs of skates, helmets, and pads and dragged everything to the side door of the warehouse. They spilled out into the basketball court and squeezed onto the one bench to lace up.

Shelly finished knotting her laces at the front, then reached for the bubble wrap roll. She began to twist it around and around her skates, adding pieces of duct tape.

Jules nudged Shelly's skate with her own. The plastic crinkled under Jules's toe stop.

"What's that?" Jules asked.

"Bubble boots," Shelly said. She fastened on her knee and elbow pads, then stood up, her arms waving. "For keeping balance."

"Right," Bree said, clipping on her helmet.

Shelly stared at the foam head left in the paper bag. She turned to Tomoko.

"All right, Tomonater," Shelly said. "The idea is that these are like laser glasses that let you see exactly where the other team's jammer is."

"Uh-huh," Tomoko said. She put on the red glasses. "The only problem is, I can't see at all."

"Really?" Shelly asked. She had imagined those infrared goggles she saw in movies that could pick out certain people from a group. Those were always red on the outside, just like Tomoko's glasses.

Shelly slipped the pair on.

"Oh wow."

The court in front of Shelly wasn't even red. It was just dark. Shelly took off the glasses and frowned at them. "I'll work on these more tonight," she said. She added them back to the bag.

Kenzie stood up and clipped on her helmet. "We're wasting time talking," she said. "Let's try out our new game plays on wheels."

Shelly waddled over to Jules and helped fasten her cloak. "Ugh, why is this so sticky?"

Jules shrugged. "I wanted to add some decoration. Otherwise it's just a gross blanket."

"It's not gross," Shelly said. She sniffed at it. "OK, so it's a little gross. But it will be flying behind you the whole time. Hey—maybe it will keep the other players away!"

Jules didn't look totally convinced.

The Daredevils lined up on the court, crouching behind an invisible blocker line. Bree waited a ways behind them.

"And go!" Shelly said. She tried to roll forward, but her bubble boots were tough to skate in. The end flaps of the packing material kept getting caught in the wheels.

Kenzie frowned at Shelly. "What game play are we trying?"

"It's a test jam," Shelly said. She grunted as she pulled her skates forward. "We're testing the new gear."

"Hmmm." Kenzie glanced at the gloves on the bench.

Bree took off from the jammer line.

Clack-clack-clack.

"Try running into me or Jules," Shelly called. Maybe her derby gear wouldn't look super cool, like the unicorn helmets. But her bubble boots and bruise prevention cloak would help her and Jules bounce right back from a fall. The Daredevils could still shine in the tournament! Shelly's gear would all make sense on the track.

Oof!

Bree slammed her hip into Shelly. Shelly barely picked

one skate up before tumbling over sideways. She landed on her back instead of her knee pads—not a good fall. She watched as Bree smacked into Jules like a bowling pin. Jules's feet flew out in front of her.

Tomoko and Kenzie swerved around and stopped.

"Well?" Bree asked. "Did they work?"

Jules looked at the blanket spread around her.

"It cushioned your fall," Shelly pointed out.

"Yeah . . ." Jules frowned. "But it's super heavy. I feel like I'd just fall more with it on."

Kenzie prodded Shelly's bubble boots. "Same with these," she said. "You can hardly move out there, Bomb Shell."

Shelly stayed very quiet. She looked at her bubble boots, then at the cushioning cloak as Jules shrugged it off. She turned to the brown paper bag with Bree's speed helmet attachment and Tomoko's laser glasses. It was starting to look like a big brown creative block.

What had happened? What went wrong?

Shelly had spent so much time building up her idea. She wasn't just drawing doodles anymore. She was making lists and collecting things. All the while her plan had gotten bigger in her head, inflating more and more until there wasn't any room for it to go wrong.

"Ugh, I can't get these off."

Shelly blinked. Tomoko was wrestling one of Shelly's skates in her lap, trying to tear off the bubble boots. "You taped it too tight," Tomoko said.

Jules reached for the scissors. "I got it!"

POP!

The tip of the scissors went into the plastic, bursting the bubble boots and Shelly's awesome plan.

CHAPTER TWELVE

SHELLY SAT ON THE BENCH FOR A LONG TIME AFTER practice was over.

The other Daredevils sat beside her. They took off their helmets and shook the sweat from their hair.

"Those new game plays are sweet," Bree said to Kenzie. "Even better in skates."

"Thanks," Kenzie said. "Tomoko really pulled off that leap-frog one."

Shelly's shoulders sagged even lower. Everything was back to the way it was before. Kenzie had the plans, Bree had the speed, Tomoko could block, Jules dished out the bruises . . . but what did Shelly have without her sketch-book? She felt like a total faker on the team.

Tomoko nudged Shelly's arm. "I'm sorry your stuff didn't

work out," she said. "But the drawings are still cool. Can you make a Tomonater picture for my room?"

"Oh," Jules said. "And maybe I can have a Crown Jules one for my locker!"

"The Bree-Zee helmet is cooler in your pictures than in real life," Bree said. "You could add some clouds to it and show me skating through the sky."

Kenzie leaned forward so she could see Shelly on the other end of the bench.

"Your drawings are really cool," Kenzie said. "We love them."

Shelly sighed and looked at her sketchbook sitting next to the bag.

"Great," Shelly muttered. Her teammates were more

excited about some pictures than the gear she had worked so hard to bring to life.

Jules popped up from the bench. "Why'd they even put a basketball hoop out here?" she asked. "No one uses the court for basketball."

"They probably did," Bree said, "before the derby league moved into the warehouse."

Tomoko finished tying her sneakers. She unzipped her bag and pulled out a basketball.

Jules's eyes went wide. "You carry that around?"

"Why not?" Tomoko said. She spun the ball on one finger. "I love basketball and derby, so I keep them both close to me!"

Tomoko flung the basketball to Jules. "One-on-one?"

Shelly, Kenzie, and Bree watched as Jules and Tomoko ran and dodged past one another on the court. Even outside of derby, Tomoko was a great blocker. Jules threw her hip into Tomoko and dribbled.

"Nice hip check!" Bree called.

Maybe Shelly didn't belong on the team. Maybe she would be better as their mascot. Or the person who brought them water. Shelly buried her face in her hands.

"You OK?" Kenzie's hand was on Shelly's back.

Shelly nodded. "Just tired." She mopped her face and watched Tomoko sink another basket.

"All right," Tomoko said. "Five to nothing. I think I'm done."

"Six out of ten!"

Bree and Kenzie laughed. Shelly mustered a small smile. She wanted to be able to laugh along with her friends. It would be so much easier if she could just forget the plan and go back to being her regular self. But the disappointment on her shoulders was so heavy—she couldn't shrug it off.

Tomoko sighed and passed the ball to Jules. "Let's play HORSE or something."

"We can play DAREDEVIL!" Jules said. She looked over at the others. "You want to play on teams?"

"You go ahead," Shelly said. "I'll just mess it up."

"How would you mess it up?" Kenzie asked. Her brows were furrowed.

Shelly shrugged. She reached for her laces.

"I'm out too," Kenzie said after a moment. "In fact, I think maybe I'll stay back with Shelly for a little bit."

Bree jumped up and put her backpack on. "Let's go shoot hoops at the park." She handed Tomoko her bag.

"Come on," Bree said. She led both Tomoko and Jules off the court and into the warehouse.

Shelly turned. She was surprised to see Kenzie still had her skates laced up.

"You're not going with them?" Shelly asked.

Kenzie shook her head. "Nah."

They sat together in silence. Over the rooftops, the sky was turning a soft pink. Shelly thought about sitting with her dad on the porch, imagining what it would be like to be a star. That felt forever ago now.

"I'm sorry," Shelly said. "I really should have gone to practice yesterday. I thought my project was going to be this awesome thing for the team. But it turned out to be a total waste."

Shelly wriggled her nose to keep the tears from climbing up.

Kenzie stared at the court. "We didn't try the gloves," she said after a moment.

Shelly turned. "Huh?"

"My Kenzilla gloves." Kenzie slipped one on her hand. "You wanted them to be sticky, right? Maybe we could try a blocking hold or something. For the tournament."

Shelly hopped up so fast that her skates nearly slipped out from under her.

"That would be so, so great," she said. Even just one thing making it to the track could hold Shelly's plan together. If the gloves worked, and the coaches saw how great Kenzie and Shelly teamed up on the court, and then realized that Shelly designed the gloves herself . . .

"Come on!" Kenzie said.

Shelly put on the other glove. Now if they held hands during a game play, they wouldn't slip!

Both girls crouched by the blocker line.

"Hey," Kenzie said. She looked at Shelly. "This is like old times."

"Yeah." Shelly smiled. "Ready?"

"Go!"

The Dynamic Duo took off around the court.

"We can try the Labyrinth play again!" Kenzie yelled. "Pretend the other jammer's coming up after us. Make a wall!"

Shelly reached out and grasped Kenzie's hand.

"This is awesome!" Shelly said. "They really stick!"

They pressed their palms tight.

"Stage two," Kenzie said. "Now we have to get ahead and form the next wall."

Shelly skated forward. Her arm jerked her back.

Kenzie wiggled her hand. "That means you have to let go."

"I'm trying!" Shelly said. She tugged her arm, but it was like she was glued to Kenzie.

"If the jammer runs into us it's a penalty!" Kenzie said. "No arm strikes, remember? We have to let go!"

Shelly grunted as she shimmied her hand. "Don't you think I know that?"

"Ow!" Kenzie said. "You're elbowing me!"

Shelly yanked her arm toward her with one quick motion.

Rip!

"Ahh!!"

Shelly and Kenzie flew

apart. Shelly tottered. She tucked her legs down and fell onto the pavement.

"Oof," Shelly said. She shook her wrist out. At least without the bubble boots she fell the right way.

Shelly sat up and looked across the court. Kenzie was on her side. She cradled one arm in front of her.

"Kenzie!" Shelly crawled on her knee pads to her friend. "Is your arm OK?"

Kenzie groaned and sat up. She peeled her Kenzilla sticky glove off and threw it down. "I think so," she said.

Shelly picked up the glove and matched it with the one she had been wearing. "I wonder if I can make a way for them to release better before tomorrow."

"What?" Kenzie unclipped her helmet. "You can't be serious."

"Well, if we want to have new gear for the tournament—"

Kenzie held up a hand. "Shelly," she said. "I stayed behind to be nice. And because you looked so sad." She pointed to Shelly's bag. "But all that stuff is junk! And worse, it's super dangerous. There's no way we can use it tomorrow."

Shelly's face got hot. "We can too!" she said. "I'm trying to help!"

Kenzie shook her head. "You sure about that?" She pulled off her skates and stood up.

Shelly watched as Kenzie grabbed her things. Kenzie didn't know what it was like to not feel special in the group. She was already the leader and planner. But new derby gear was all Shelly had. It was her only chance at Star Skater.

"Maybe I'll just stand out without you! Maybe I'll show off all by myself!" Shelly called.

Kenzie paused at the warehouse door. "Maybe you will," she said.

The side door rattled as it banged shut, leaving Shelly on the court all alone.

CHAPTER THIRTEEN

SHELLY USUALLY ONLY SPENT SUNDAY AND MONDAY nights with her dad, but that evening her mom was guest-teaching a painting class downtown. Shelly's dad showed up in the warehouse parking lot. His eyes got big as Shelly dragged the giant paper bag behind her, but he lifted it right up and carried it the rest of the way to his workshop. Shelly tipped the bag over in front of her dad's tool bench, digging all of her broken designs out.

"Hoo boy. Looks like you got your work cut out for you, kiddo," her dad said. He and Shelly folded their arms and surveyed the pile of stuff. "Is this for a school project?"

Shelly shook her head. "It's for derby," she said. "I have to fix it or else I won't have a shot at being Star Skater in the tournament."

Shelly took out the Tomonater glasses. "Like, I wanted these to be red," she said, scraping the paint away. "But the paint just made everything go dark."

"Here." Shelly's dad fished through a drawer in his tool bench, then handed Shelly a thin sheet of plastic. "It has a red tint. And you can cut it to fit the frames."

Shelly held the plastic in front of her. "Oh yeah, this is much better."

She picked up the blanket. It was still sticky from where Jules had glued the confetti on.

"This was supposed to be a cloak," Shelly said dejectedly.

Her dad held up a roll of thick cord. "You need a better way to tie that together."

"And make it shorter," Shelly said. "Hey! Maybe we can cut a piece to go around the hips. And it can be a hip-bumper for protecting against bruises."

"Now you're thinking," her dad said. He nudged Shelly's shoulder.

One by one, Shelly went through her list. She painted the Kenzilla gloves green and took off one set of sticky pads so they would come apart easier. She found two tiny propellers in the workshop and decided to make them into skate boosters for Bree-Zee instead of the helmet attachment. She made the pouch for her exploding wrist guards again and again, adding in more air and less confetti. She practiced with them until finally, she clapped and the confetti went everywhere! Shelly remade the pouch one last time and attached it to her left wrist guard. The explosion could only happen once, but it would still impress everyone.

Shelly's dad checked his watch.

"Getting late," he said. "What do you say we head upstairs?"

Shelly pressed her lips together. There was still something missing. She leaned over the bag, staring at something glinting from the bottom.

"Can we stay down here a little longer? I want to make a couple more things."

Her dad smiled. "Just tell me what to do."

Shelly didn't play the lava game on her way to the warehouse the next day. Her feet were too tired to pick up and hop around. She shuffled down the sidewalk and across parking lots. The empty squares of pavement stretched on like blank pages. Maybe if Shelly weren't so sleepy, she would draw imaginary squiggles in the squares, and then turn those imaginary squiggles into imaginary full pictures that danced and swirled. But Shelly only yawned and heaved her bag onward.

She shoved herself through the warehouse doors. Inside, junior league teams were already zooming in loops around the track. Shelly scanned the bleachers. The rest of the Daredevils were already here too. They even had their gear on. Shelly scrunched up her face. Were they meeting without her?

She went to the row where the other Daredevils were sitting.

"Um, hi."

Bree looked up. "Whoa. You look kind of awful."

"Thanks," Shelly said.

"You just look tired," Tomoko said. "Did you stay up late?"

Shelly stood in front of the bag. One handle was barely hanging on.

"And got up early," she said. A yawn escaped before she could stop it.

"My mom calls that burning the candle at both ends," Jules said. "It's like setting both your feet and your hair on fire."

Shelly rolled her eyes. She noticed Kenzie was bent over one skate, tying and untying the laces.

"Did you all meet here without me?" Shelly asked.

Kenzie sat up. "We figured you might be busy with your own stuff."

Shelly winced. She didn't like feeling left out. But soon everyone would see what she was working on.

"Actually," she said, "I spent all night fixing everything." She reached into the bag and pulled out the skate propellers, then set them in front of Bree. Bree hardly glanced at the propellers before she looked away.

"No thanks," Bree said. She finished wrapping her wrist guard.

Shelly sat on the bench. "It's to give your skates a boost. You know, Bree-Zee, fast like a breeze?"

"She said she doesn't want to wear them," Kenzie said. Her voice was low and quiet.

Shelly looked around. Everyone seemed to inch farther away from her.

She slumped her shoulders and turned to get her skates from the rental counter. They had the yellow spot on the

wheel, like always. By the time she got back to the bench, the other Daredevils were sliding onto the rink for practice laps. The propellers sat alone.

Fffttt!

A loud whistle cut through the warehouse. The skaters on the rink stopped. Shelly finished knotting her laces and stood up. She clomped across the carpet and skated to the jammer line, where Mambo Rambo, Razzle Dazzle, and Look Out were waiting. Shelly took a place behind the rest of the Daredevils.

"Welcome to your first official tournament," Mambo said. Her eyes were wide and smiley, like she expected everyone to dance around again.

Shelly stole glances at the other teams. A few people clapped, but almost everyone looked nervous. Suddenly, a tournament felt like a very big deal.

Raz gave a particularly loud *whoop!* She looked down at her clipboard. "We've got five Austin teams going against three teams from New Mexico. That means the Taco Bout-its and Shady Birds will be going head to head."

The two Austin teams twisted around and looked each other over.

"Let's meet our visiting teams," Lo said. "Introducing the Albuquerque, New Mexico, junior league!"

Lo threw her arm with a flourish toward the side door. Fifteen girls came streaming inside. Everyone wore normal-looking skates and helmets. Shelly blinked. Where were the unicorn horns from the picture?

Raz motioned for the Austin league to stand up. Shelly scrambled in line and high-fived the New Mexico teams as they stepped onto the track.

"We're going to have a great time today," Mambo said to everyone. "Go ahead and get changed into your tournament gear in the locker rooms! New Mexico league, your locker room is over this way."

Shelly grabbed her things and followed the others. Everything seemed to be happening so fast. Had the Daredevils practiced enough? Did they have game plays for every kind of jam? What if the other teams outsmarted them? Or were faster? Or meaner? Shelly squeezed the propellers. Her derby gear had seemed like a clear path to shine, but now it seemed like her last bit of hope.

The Daredevils settled in the far corner of the locker room.

"Everyone have knee pads, elbow pads, and wrist guards?" Kenzie asked.

"Yep," Jules said. She patted her leg. "And a good set of bruises to match!"

Shelly started to dig around in her bag. "Actually, I made something for that."

"I told you," Kenzie said. "The team decided. We're sticking with basic gear only."

The fuzzy hip bumper fell from Shelly's grip. "But—"

"OK! Game play time!" Kenzie clapped her hands. Bree, Tomoko, and Jules leaned in.

Shelly's empty hand balled into a fist at her side. She sat with her back turned to the others.

As the Daredevils whispered about plays, Shelly crossed her arms and watched the other teams. The Cow Pokes were doing a cheer. The Cherry Pits threw on their signature shirts. The other teams looked so cool, all dressing alike. Shelly glanced at her bag.

Raz stuck her head in the door. "We're ready out there! First up, the Daredevils!"

Shelly's eyebrows shot up. They were going *first*?

The chatter and giggling in the locker room quieted down. Shelly and the others slowly stood up from their corner.

"Here we go," Bree whispered.

As Shelly watched her teammates file through the locker room, she leaned toward her bag and snatched both the propellers and her special wrist guard. Wearing her gear by herself hadn't been Shelly's original plan, but it was the last chance she had to prove herself to the team. With skate boosters and a hidden flash of confetti, Shelly was sure to stand out on the track.

CHAPTER FOURTEEN

ONE BY ONE, THE DAREDEVILS SQUEEZED OUT OF THE locker room. The warehouse barely looked like it did during normal practice. The high spotlights shone down over the rink. Shelly could see heads bobbing everywhere in the stands. Somewhere on those benches, her parents were watching. Her palms were slick with sweat.

The girls spread out on one of the official team benches along the sidelines.

A man dressed in a giant flamingo costume waltzed onto the rink. He cleared his throat and leaned into the microphone.

"Ladies and gentlemen, lone wolves and cuttlefish," he said, "thank you for attending the first ever Austin vs. Albuquerque junior league tournament!"

Everyone sitting in the bleachers clapped.

"What does that mean?" Tomoko whispered. "Lone wolves and cuttlefish?"

"The announcer always adds something with 'ladies and gentlemen,'" Kenzie explained, "because not everyone fits in just those two categories."

Shelly nodded. "Like my friend Fen," she said. She remembered what Fen had said in the craft store about teamwork. They would definitely be more of a cuttlefish than a lone wolf.

"For our first bout," the announcer continued, "we have the Austin Derby Daredevils up against the Albuquerque Brawling Dolls!"

The crowd cheered again.

Bree leaned in toward the others. "Ooh, that look is creepy."

The Daredevils turned over their shoulders as the first team stood up from the sidelines. Shelly gulped. While the fifteen girls she had high-fived all looked like regular kids, the Brawling Dolls now wore matching blue dresses over leggings. They also painted around their eyes and cheeks, and looked exactly like zombie dolls sprung to life.

"Sweet uniforms," Jules said. "We should have painted our faces!"

"Yeah," Tomoko said. "We should have done something for our team look."

Shelly bit her lip. She thought about the things sitting in her paper bag in the locker room.

The Daredevils rose from the bench together and got ready to follow the Brawling Dolls onto the track. Shelly tugged her wrist guard into place and clipped the propellers to her skates.

"What are you doing?" Kenzie asked.

"You don't have to wear my stuff," Shelly said. "But it's awesome, and I'm wearing it anyway. You'll see."

Tomoko stood next to Kenzie. She pointed at the propellers. "What if you hurt someone?"

"They're made out of foam!" Shelly said. "They won't hurt anyone." She brushed by her teammates and sailed toward the blocker line. Tomoko and Kenzie skated quietly after her.

Shelly took her place between the Brawling Dolls. One of the blockers glanced at Shelly's skates uneasily. Shelly smiled. Maybe her plan would still work.

"Pack—go!"

Look Out blew the whistle. Shelly took off with the rest of the blockers. She bumped elbows with Kenzie, which would usually make the girls turn and smile at each other. But today, neither one smiled.

"Jammers—go!"

Lo blew the whistle again. This time Bree and the Brawling Dolls jammer took off from the jammer line. Mambo and Raz, who were acting as jammer referees, skated along the sidelines, watching to see which jammer would make it through the pack first. That jammer would be the "lead," or the person who got to decide when the jam was over.

Since Shelly didn't know what game play the Daredevils were doing, she decided to carve a gap in the pack for Bree to get through. The *clacking* of Bree's skates got closer. Shelly slammed her hip into a Dolls blocker.

"Umph," the blocker said.

Shelly grinned. But then something tugged on her foot. She looked down. Her propeller had gotten stuck in the blocker's skate!

"Oh, no," Shelly said. She tried to pull her skate free.

Fffttt!

Lo blew her whistle. Both teams came to a stop.

"Foreign object on the track!" Lo called.

Shelly slowly looked behind her. The now-mangled propeller sat in the middle of the rink.

"What is that?" Mambo asked.

Jules kicked the propeller away. "I think it's a dead bug!" she called.

One of the Brawling Dolls spoke up.

"It tripped me during the jam," she said. "It came from *her* skate. See? There's another one!"

Shelly hunched her shoulders. She wanted to crawl under a rock and hide.

Raz skated over to Shelly. She squatted down and pulled the propeller from Shelly's other skate.

"What's this, Bomb Shell?"

"Skate boosters?" Shelly said. She was so nervous, her voice went high like she was the one asking a question.

Raz shook her head. "Dress code mandate two point six: Accessories can't interfere with the function or safety of basic derby gear. That means skates. I'll give you a warning, but if anything else interferes with the jam, it's a major penalty. Got it?"

Shelly's cheeks were on fire. "Got it."

"All good!" Raz called. "Restart!"

The eight blockers skated back to the pack line. Kenzie glanced at Shelly. She almost looked like she felt sorry for her. But Shelly couldn't make herself meet Kenzie's eyes. She couldn't look at anyone. The best she could do was blend into the group and not get in any more trouble.

"Restart—pack—go!"

"Restart—jammers—go!"

Shelly did her best to stay in stride with everyone else.

She still didn't know the Daredevils' blocking strategy, and she was too embarrassed to hip check another Dolls blocker. Shelly kept her arms pinned down at her sides. The pouch in her wrist guard dug into her skin.

Clack-clack-clack.

That was Bree.

Shelly took a breath. All she had to do was get out of the way, and Bree could pass. Shelly shifted and leaned into her right skate. Then Bree would slip on the inside and make lead jammer.

"Mmph!" A Brawling Dolls blocker shoved Bree into Shelly's shoulder. Shelly tried to press Bree forward in the pack. But the other jammer hip checked Bree hard.

Bree went sailing for Shelly's left side.

"No!" Shelly yelled.

FOOM!

Every skater dug their toe stops into the track. The entire warehouse went quiet. All eyes turned to Bree and Shelly, who were covered in confetti.

Ffftttt!

This time both Raz and Mambo skated on either side of Shelly. They rummaged in the fanny packs slung across their black-and-white jerseys. Bree and Shelly watched as Raz took out a red card while Mambo took out a yellow one.

Raz shook her head. "I already gave Bomb Shell a warning," she said. "She's out."

"Out?" Bree's eyebrows shot up. "As in out of the game?"

Shelly felt a pinch in her nose. Her eyes were blurry. How could this be happening? Her gear was supposed to show everyone how great she was, not get her thrown from the bout!

"The warning was for skate interference," Mambo said.

"It was for distracting accessories." Raz waved the red card again.

Mambo pointed to the official table, where the coaches from the New Mexico league sat behind two clipboards. "You wrote it down as skate interference."

Suddenly Lo stood between the referees. "Do we have a consensus?" Lo asked. She glanced at Raz and Mambo, then the yellow and red cards.

"Referee deliberation! Time-out: Two minutes."

Ffftttt!

As soon as the whistle dropped from Lo's mouth, Shelly broke away from the others and flew off the track.

She had wanted to bring her sketches to life to help the team. She thought her wrist guard might even earn her the Star Skater title. But as she ducked into the locker room, tears flowing, Shelly realized it was about to earn her a one-way ticket out of the tournament.

CHAPTER FIFTEEN

SHELLY PUSHED THE DOOR TO THE LOCKER ROOM SO hard that the handle knocked into the wall. The other Austin league teams jolted upright.

"It's over already?" one player asked. "Y'all just started!"

Shelly didn't say anything. She rolled to the far corner where the Daredevils had stashed their bags. Shelly crouched against a locker bay and curled into a ball.

The door squeaked open again.

"Um, Shelly?"

Shelly looked up. Jules leaned into the room. "The time-out's supposed to be on the team benches."

"I'll be there in a minute," Shelly said.

She sniffed. She wasn't sure she would be coming back out. Shelly remembered the roller derby tryouts a month earlier. When Camila quit the team, they almost had to forfeit before Bree joined. Was that going to happen now? Would Shelly's stupid exploding wrist guard yank the whole team from the tournament?

"We said you had a bloody nose," Bree said. Her head popped up behind Jules's. "That bought us another five minutes."

Jules and Bree skated into the room, followed closely by Tomoko and Kenzie. Shelly wiped her eyes with her sleeve. She could feel the other teams staring her down.

"What happened?" someone whispered.

"What happened is the derby player seats are all empty waiting for you," Bree said. "We need a cheer section out there! Come on."

The other four teams mumbled as they shifted and pulled one another up. The Daredevils stood, waiting, until every last person slid out of the locker room.

Tomoko turned to Shelly. "Why'd you come back here, Bomb Shell?"

Shelly dropped her legs down. She tried to sit up taller.

"I had to get off the track," Shelly said. "I just wanted to . . . I don't know, disappear."

Kenzie raised an eyebrow. "Disappear? Why?"

Jules and Bree sat next to Shelly against the lockers.

"Because trying to stand out led to this," Shelly said. She brushed some confetti off of her shirt. "They're going to throw me out of the tournament. And it's all my fault."

Bree helped Shelly take off her wrist guard. The deflated plastic pouch fell onto Shelly's lap.

"The confetti thing was an accident," Bree said. "I ran into you—you didn't set it off. The refs won't take you out for that."

"They might," Shelly said. She stared at the wrinkled plastic and sighed. "I don't know. Maybe they should. I don't deserve to be on the track."

Kenzie shook her head. "That confetti explosion must have messed with you. You're not thinking clearly."

Shelly reached over Jules's lap and threw the empty pouch into her brown paper bag.

"I wasn't thinking clearly before," Shelly said. "I wasn't thinking about the other players on the track. I wasn't thinking about you guys when I missed Thursday's practice. I was just thinking about myself, really. And how bad I wanted to win Star Skater."

Jules cocked her head. "Star Skater?"

"I saw it on the tournament poster," Shelly said.

"They're giving the award to one player. I thought if my derby gear worked, and I got the award, then you would see how important I was."

"Hold up a sec." Bree scooted away from Shelly so she could look at her head-on. "You think we don't know how important you are?"

Shelly shrugged.

"I mean . . . you're the fastest, Bree. And Kenzie, you're the one in charge of game plays. Tomoko blocks better than everyone else. And Jules collects and dishes out more bruises than any of us."

"You do all those things too," Kenzie said. "You're really fast. You plan moves with me. You're a great blocker. And I've gotten some gnarly bruises from your hip checks."

"But I'm not the best in any of them," Shelly said. "You're like an all-star team. And then there's me."

"Nuh-uh," Bree said. "Such lies. Bomb Shell, you single-handedly got me through the pack back there."

"Our plays don't work without you," Kenzie said. "We need you."

Shelly clamped down on her lip. What if the others were just being nice?

"Hey." Jules leaned into the paper bag. "What's this?"

"The rest of the gear." Shelly tugged Jules's shirt. "Don't worry about that."

"No," Jules said. "I mean what's *this*?"

She pulled a piece of sparkling purple fabric from the bag. The light bounced off the sequins and onto the Daredevils' faces.

"Oh," Shelly said. "I made uniforms to go with the gear."

Jules stretched the fabric. "Is it a tube?"

"It's a sleeve," Shelly said.

Jules took off her wrist guard and elbow pad. Shelly helped shimmy the material over Jules's arm.

"I cut it up from an old leotard," Shelly said. "Camila found it in the costume room at school."

"Camila?" Bree asked. "You mean the girl from tryouts?"

"Yeah," Shelly said. "She's really cool. She does back-stage theater stuff."

"The costume crypt is the *coolest*," Jules said. "I remember that place. They never let the actors go down there."

Tomoko touched the sequins over Jules's sleeve. "I love this. I want one."

Shelly fished out the second purple sleeve and handed it to Jules. She rooted through the bag and took out two red sequined sleeves.

"For you," she said to Tomoko. "I made a set for everyone. I also made cut-outs."

Shelly dropped several scraps of red material onto Tomoko's lap. "They're supposed to look like robot buttons," Shelly said. "You know, for the Tomonater. There's sticky stuff on the back so you can attach them to your knee pads."

"Oh wow." Tomoko slapped the red circles onto her knees. "This is awesome!"

Shelly smiled. "Really?"

"Gimme mine!" Bree said.

Shelly leaned into the bag and took out a purple crown cut-out she made for Jules's helmet. She then took out blue sleeves for Bree along with two cloud cut-outs for Bree's wrist guards. She found her own yellow sleeves and the explosion cut-outs for her elbow pads. Shelly pulled Kenzie's green sequined sleeves out last, along with two strips of the green material cut into claw shapes.

"They're supposed to stick onto your skates," Shelly said. She left them on the floor in front of Kenzie. "For Kenzilla feet. If you want them, I mean."

Kenzie stared at the green pile.

"You don't have to wear any of it," Shelly said. "I was just trying to make something cool for the team. I'm sorry I missed your practice and made you wear those gloves. I'm sorry I was selfish."

At last Kenzie looked up. "I'm sorry too," she said. "I kind of blew off your ideas last week for being too silly. But being silly is part of our team's charm!"

She reached out and squeezed Shelly's hand.

The Daredevils slipped on their sleeves. Jules placed the

crown cut-out around her helmet. Bree smoothed the cloud shapes over her wrist guards. Kenzie attached the claw cut-outs onto her skates. Tomoko lined up her red buttons to look like a killer robot. Shelly wrapped the yellow-sequined explosions around her elbow pads.

The team crowded over the sinks and checked themselves out in the mirror.

"We look like a sparkling rainbow of destruction," Jules said. She swiped her arm through the air. "Hi-yah!"

"We look like an all-star team," Kenzie said. "All of us."

The door to the locker room opened again.

"OK, Daredevils," Lo said. "Time in. Bomb Shell, we need you in the ref circle."

CHAPTER SIXTEEN

SHELLY GULPED.

"Coming."

She skated through the doorway after Lo. Mambo and Raz were waiting on the rink.

"Wait!" Bree threw the door open. "I'm coming too."

Bree slid onto the track and did a toe-stop right next to Shelly. "I got pushed into Shelly," Bree said. "So if she's out, then we're both out."

"Me three!" Jules stumbled across the carpet. "I'll go out!"

"Don't forget about us!" Kenzie and Tomoko glided onto the track with their team.

The announcer tugged his flamingo cap down and clicked

the microphone on. "Is it just me or have these Daredevils powered up?" he asked.

Some of the people in the bleachers clapped.

Mambo raised an eyebrow. "What happened back there?"

Kenzie shrugged. "We forgot our uniforms before," she said. "We figured while you were deliberating we could get dressed."

"Yeah," Jules said. "And we look good from all angles, even the sidelines if you bench us!"

Raz looked surprised. "Why would we bench you?"

"Because of me," Shelly said. "I'm the one who brought

the skate boosters, and the confetti came out of my wrist guard. So if you want to take me out, you should take just me. But can't the others stay in the tournament?"

Mambo and Raz looked at each other.

"Bomb Shell," Raz said. "Going out means sitting in the penalty box for a minute while your team continues the jam. That's what a major penalty is."

"Oh," Shelly said. She turned to her teammates. "Well . . . that seems fair."

The other Daredevils shrugged and nodded.

"We'll be able to fend the Brawling Dolls off for a minute," Tomoko said. She smiled. "Barely, though."

Shelly tipped her helmet to her teammates. "To the penalty box!" she said.

Lo led Shelly over to a chair labeled MAJOR PENALTY. It wasn't inside of a box at all, which was a little disappointing. But at least Shelly could watch her teammates and cheer them on.

"Yeah Daredevils!" Shelly called. "Go get 'em!"

The starting whistle blew and the pack of blockers took off. Shelly watched as Kenzie leaned into the other blockers. Kenzie held up four fingers to Bree, who was coming up behind them. It was an older play Shelly recognized. The four was actually American Sign Language for the letter "B," which meant the Daredevils' Backward game play.

In the Backward play, Bree would call out one move, like "pass left!" or "block right!" and the blockers would do the exact opposite. That way, if the other team tried to stop them, they would have no idea what the Daredevils were really doing.

"Passing on the right!" Bree called, which meant she was going to try to pass on the left instead.

Tomoko and Jules swayed to the right, pinning the Brawling Dolls jammer behind them. The Dolls blockers looked around for Bree. Then one of the blockers saw Bree over her shoulder.

They know what Bree's doing, Shelly thought.

Bree tried to slip behind the turned heads, but the Brawling Dolls blocker came charging for her. Shelly was usually the blocker on the inside of the pack. If she were there, Bree could have a clear shot at lead jammer.

Oof!

The blocker hip checked into Bree's side. Tomoko turned

to help Bree. The Dolls jammer squeezed past Tomoko and shot forward.

"Lead jammer—Brawling Dolls!" Raz called.

Shelly was on the edge of her seat. Bree dug through the blockers and was right behind the Brawling Dolls jammer. The two jammers looped around the rink. They were heading for the pack. Kenzie made the "B" sign.

Again? Shelly shook her head. The Brawling Dolls already knew what they were up to. The Dolls jammer wasn't hard to keep back, but the blockers had it out for Bree. The Daredevils had to focus on helping their own jammer.

"Head forward!" Bree said. That meant she wanted the Daredevils blockers to stay at the back of the pack.

Tomoko curved her skates in, and this time she saw the Brawling Dolls blocker waiting for Bree. But the Dolls jammer shot right by her. Kenzie and Jules sprung in front of the jammer.

Fffttt!

"End jam. Brawling Dolls: two points, Daredevils: zero." Lo held up two fingers on one hand and made the other into a fist. She blew the whistle again and waved at Shelly. "Daredevils blocker Bomb Shell, back in!"

Shelly shot up from the penalty box and raced to her team.

Everyone, even Bree, was waiting for her at the pack line.

Kenzie knocked Shelly's helmet. "Glad you're back, Bomb Shell," she said.

"We need you!" Bree added. "I'm getting pummeled out there."

Shelly leaned in. "I was watching," she said. "And the Brawling Dolls jammer isn't too hard to handle. Tomonater, think you can take her this next jam?"

Tomoko nodded. "Can do."

"Great," Shelly said. "That leaves the three of us to help Bree."

"What are you thinking?" Jules asked.

Shelly smiled. "Three words: Flying. Circle. Doom."

Bree pumped her arm. "Yes!"

"All right," Kenzie said. "I like it."

The girls threw their hands together.

"What are we?" Bree yelled.

"Dare—"

"Devils!"

Shelly tossed her hand high and stood between Kenzie and Jules. She took a deep breath in, then out. She hoped the game play would work.

Lo signaled the pack. "Jam two—pack, go!"

Shelly skated in line with Kenzie and Jules. Left skate, right skate, just like they practiced. The three blockers joined hands. The jammers were coming behind them.

"Ready?" Kenzie asked.

Jules and Shelly nodded.

"Caw-caw! Caw-caw!" the three cried.

Kenzie and Jules let their hands go just as Bree got to the pack. They clasped hands again behind her. Kenzie and Shelly leaned forward and grabbed hold of each other's hands. Now Bree was inside the circle.

"Caw-caw!"

"What are you doing?" a Brawling Dolls blocker yelled.

"Flying Circle of Doom!" Shelly answered.

Shelly, Kenzie, and Jules pushed Bree toward the front edge of the pack. Kenzie and Shelly dropped their handhold and Bree shot forward.

"Lead jammer—Daredevils!" Mambo said.

Shelly grinned.

"All right!"

She bumped fists with Kenzie and then Jules. Maybe Shelly wasn't the smartest planner or the best blocker, but when it came to plays like the Flying Circle of Doom, the Daredevils couldn't do things without her.

CHAPTER SEVENTEEN

"END JAM. DAREDEVILS: FOUR POINTS, BRAWLING Dolls: two points."

"That's four to four total," Tomoko said. "We're really in it now!"

Kenzie signaled everyone to huddle. The Daredevils put their heads together, coming up with new plays for every jam. They used their Crying Banshee move and their Labyrinth move. Over halftime, Kenzie even came up with some new game plays for the team to try.

"Jam seven!"

"Jam ten!"

"End jam eleven," Lo called. "Daredevils: two points, Brawling Dolls: two points. Last jam—set."

"Daredevils," Kenzie said. "We're only down by three.

We need to get Bree through the whole pack and stop the Dolls jammer."

"What's your plan?" Tomoko asked.

Shelly leaned in.

"The Madame President," Kenzie said, her eyebrows wiggling. The Madame President was one of the Daredevils' newest plays. They had never tried it out on wheels before.

"Usually we only have two security guards," Kenzie said. "But I think in this case, we'll need three to get Bree through. Tomoko, mind handling the other jammer on your own again?"

"Wait." Shelly waved. "Can I take the jammer?"

Tomoko's eyes widened. "You want to?"

"Yeah," Shelly said. She tightened her hands into fists. "I can do it."

Kenzie patted Shelly's shoulder. "We believe in you, Bomb Shell!"

Shelly smiled. When the blockers broke the huddle and got in line, Shelly felt ready. She would shift her hips back and forth, the way Tomoko did on the track. She would throw herself into hip checks like Jules. She would stay in front of the jammer and outskate her. She would outsmart the other team. It was all going to come together.

"Jam twelve—pack, go!"

Shelly skated alongside the pack. This time she didn't want to disappear into the group. She didn't want to stand away from her team either. Shelly waved her arms, letting the lights bounce off her yellow-sequined sleeves. She wanted the audience to see she was a Daredevil, and she deserved to be there.

Clack-clack-clack.

Bree was coming fast. Shelly turned and watched as Kenzie, Jules, and Tomoko put a hand to their ear, the way they had seen the Secret Service do for the president. They threw their arms out and made way for Bree to get through.

Click-clack, click-clack.

That was the sound of the other jammer's skates. Shelly took a deep breath and braced herself. The jammer wasn't so hard to block. She had seen Tomoko take her on again and again. Shelly knew could do it too.

"Argh," Shelly grunted. She swished her hips from side to side.

But the jammer kept swerving around Shelly. Shelly had to pump her arms and legs to catch up.

"Hi-yah!" Shelly said. She tried to aim a hip check for the jammer.

But the jammer moved out of the way. Shelly was going to lose her! Shelly dove for the jammer again.

"Backup!" someone called.

Suddenly Jules was next to Shelly.

"Double trouble!" Jules yelled.

Shelly looked over. "What?"

Jules didn't answer. She hurtled forward. Shelly followed until they were on either side of the Brawling Dolls jammer. Jules leaned her hip out, and Shelly understood. She leaned her hip out too.

"Hi-yah!" Jules threw her hip into the jammer. This time, the jammer stumbled. Shelly waited, then bumped her again on the other hip. The jammer fell back.

"Lead jammer—Daredevils!"

Jules gave a karate chop to the air. "Hi-yah! We did it!" She grinned at Shelly.

Shelly wanted to grin back, but for some reason she didn't feel like smiling. They had stopped the jammer just like she'd wanted to. But Tomoko hadn't needed backup. Why couldn't Shelly do things as well as the others? Something sour settled in the pit of Shelly's stomach.

Ffftttt!

The announcer took hold of the microphone.

"And that's our first bout!" he called. "The final score is twenty-four to twenty-three, with the Daredevils snatching that lead in the final jam! Let's give a huge round of applause to the Brawling Dolls for coming to life and knocking the cabbage patch right out of us! And give a huge round to the Daredevils for setting the track a-whirlin'!"

The audience in the stands whooped and cheered. The Brawling Dolls and Daredevils lined up on either side of the track. They held their arms out and high-fived one another.

"Good bout!" the Dolls called. "Good bout! Nice skating."

"Good job boxing me out," Bree told the one Dolls blocker. "You made passes almost impossible."

"You found a way through," the Dolls blocker said, smiling.

"Nice uniforms," the Dolls jammer said. "They were super distracting. But in a good way."

Kenzie nudged Shelly.

"Oh," Shelly said. She looked up from the floor. "Thanks."

The two teams made their way to the stands where the other skaters sat.

"Are we skating again?" Tomoko asked Razzle Dazzle.

Raz shook her head. "Nah, we only have time for four bouts, so every team can play once. Good job, though, y'all!" She jabbed Jules's elbow playfully.

The Daredevils scooted down one slat of bleachers until they were all sitting in a row. Another Austin league team, the Cow Pokes, scrambled up and onto the track. The New Mexico unicorn team stood up as well. They were wearing their horns, just like in the picture. But one by one, each player pulled her horn off and left it in her seat before she took to the track. Tomoko was right; the horns were detachable.

Shelly propped her chin in her hand as she watched the next three bouts unfold between the Cow Pokes vs. the Unicorns, the Taco Bout-its vs. the Shady Birds, and the Cherry Pits vs. the Block 'Em Sock 'Em Ro-bouts. She watched the teams come together for different plays. She watched them split up the work, taking on different blockers and jammers on their own. She watched the really fast jammers, the tough hip-checkers, and the blockers who paddled jammers back and forth like they were playing Ping-Pong.

Shelly sighed. The Daredevils said she was important to the team. But still, there wasn't anything Shelly was *best* at. She was more like the team helper.

Ffftttt!

Look Out blew the whistle on the fourth and final bout.

"And the Cherry Pits sweep up the win with a handy thirty points!" the announcer crooned. "Give a hand to the Block 'Em Sock 'Em Ro-bouts, who definitely rocked the

Pits around the rink. And give a hand to the Cherry Pits, for bringing back one heck of a sour punch!"

Shelly and the others stood and cheered. The teams on the track high-fived. They came back to the stands and squished in with the others.

Mambo Rambo stepped next to the microphone and whispered to the announcer.

"Huh?"

The announcer pulled back his flamingo cap. He cupped his ear and leaned in toward Mambo. "Oh, right! The Austin league coaches have conferred and would like to award today's Star Skater title to Loriel Pacheco from the Brawling Dolls!"

The Dolls blocker who had been on Bree's tail throughout the bout stood up from the stands. The other skaters clapped her on the back and pumped their arms over and over. Bree stuck two fingers in her mouth and whistled. Shelly clapped too. The blocker had been really good—definitely the best on her team. It made sense that she won.

As Loriel stepped onto the rink, Mambo took out a necklace with a glittery gold star and threaded it over Loriel's shoulders. Loriel smiled and blushed, then turned for the stands.

"Hold on a second there," the announcer called.

"The Albuquerque coaches have also made their choice for Star Skater from the Austin league." The announcer raised one of his bright-pink flamingo wings. "Molly Moorgan from the Cherry Pits!"

Shelly made her hands smack together over and over as Molly joined Loriel on the rink. She watched as the two Star Skaters waved and showed off their prizes. She turned and gazed at all the other skaters still sitting next to her on the stands.

Everyone worked so hard in the tournament, Shelly realized. But they couldn't all be Star Skaters. Shelly picked at the explosion cutouts on her elbow pads. She knew she was a good skater too. But maybe she just wasn't meant to stand out.

CHAPTER EIGHTEEN

AFTER THE CHEERS AND CLAPPING DIED DOWN, BOTH Star Skaters turned and sat back in the stands.

"Well, we're all out of stars," the announcer said. He waved a slip of paper. "But I do have one more name here."

Shelly looked down at her laces. She held her hands a few inches apart, ready to make them clap again.

The announcer peered at the note. "Thanks to all who voted, the viewers' choice for Best Team Uniform goes to . . . the Daredevils!"

Shelly froze. Her hands didn't move. She looked up.

"That's us!" Shelly said.

Bree threw her arm around Shelly's side. "That's *you*!"

The Daredevils screamed and cheered and stomped their skates.

Shelly rose from the bench. Her knee pads were shaking. She made it to the end of the bleacher row, then turned to her teammates.

"Come on!" she said.

Kenzie grinned and rolled after Shelly. Bree was behind her, Tomoko behind her, and Jules made another "Hi-yah!" as she skated onto the rink.

Shelly stood next to the announcer. She looked out into the audience and beamed. Her parents were sitting together, waving at her.

"Daredevils," the announcer said, "what made you choose to have different uniforms instead of the same one?"

He passed the microphone down to Shelly.

"Well," Shelly said, "even though we're all Daredevils, each one of us is really different. We wanted to stand out, but also come together on the track."

"I'll say!" the announcer spoke into the mic again. "Let's have one more round for the viewers' choice, as well as every skater here who played their darn tootin' hearts out this afternoon!"

"Wooooo!"

The Daredevils skated to the bleachers and pulled the next row of skaters up from their seats. Soon all eight junior league teams were bowing and waving and dancing over the track. The announcer flapped his wings and stepped aside. Music blared out from the speakers.

"Hey!" Tomoko said. "We look like disco balls!"

Jules held her arms out and spun around in circles. She made it three times before falling over.

"Or strobe lights," Bree said. "*Bom-che, bom-che, bom-che, bom-che.*"

Kenzie and Shelly pumped their hands up and down. They wiggled and linked arms and did the robot next to Tomoko.

Soon all the friends and families in the stands were making their way onto the track. Shelly's mom and dad waited for Shelly to skate over. Her mom bent down and gave Shelly a hug.

"I'm so proud of you, Shell," she said. "Your designs really came together!"

"Yeah," Shelly said. She looked at her dad sheepishly. "Some of them."

Her dad grinned and pulled Shelly into a big bear hug of his own. "You did awesome, Bomb Shell," he said. He held Shelly away from him and looked her over. "In fact . . . I think you're carrying on your dad's old nickname."

"I am?" Shelly asked. But she didn't win a glittery star.

"I'd say so, Miss Shiny!" Shelly's dad pointed at the sequined uniforms on all the Daredevils.

Shelly looked around, a slow smile spreading across her face as she watched her teammates shimmer under the lights. Shelly *was* shiny, but not like her dad. She was shiny in her own special way.

Kenzie and her family shuffled over to Shelly and her parents.

"I hear you're the designer!" Kenzie's dad said. "Congratulations, Bomb Shell!"

"The Hazel Nuts could use your eye with our own look," Kenzie's mom said. "We're overdue for a team makeover before our next bout."

Shelly blushed. "Thanks, Ms. E."

The other Daredevils and their families gathered

around. Kenzie's dad hoisted Kenzie's little sister, Verona, on his hip.

"Speaking of being overdue," Kenzie's dad said, "I think we owe you kids a celebration dinner! Who's up for some tacos?"

All the Daredevils—and Shelly's dad—raised their hands. Shelly laughed as she took off her skates and turned them in to the rental counter. The crew met back in the locker room and carefully peeled off their sleeves. Instead of shoving them back into the paper bag, each member folded the sequined material and placed it into her own bag or backpack. They followed their families out of the warehouse and into a perfect, warm Austin afternoon.

Everyone spread over the sidewalk in clusters as they walked down South Congress to the taco stand. The Daredevils gathered at their own table. Shelly's dad brought an armload of fizzy water for the girls to guzzle down as they waited for their tacos.

Shelly had just brought the bottle to her lips when she heard a light *tink-tink-tink* against glass. She set her water down and looked across at Kenzie, who was tapping her nail against her own glass bottle.

"Attention," Kenzie said, but she only said it loud enough for the five Daredevils to hear. "I think we need some more official dubbing in the group."

"But we already have derby names!" Tomoko said.

"Yeah," Jules added. "And also, if anyone's doing dubbing around here, it should be the Crown Jules!"

Kenzie laughed. "OK, Crown Jules," she said. "You be the one to dub, then. Thanks to some great points made by Bomb Shell, I think we all deserve some official titles."

Shelly clutched her bottle. "We do?"

"Yep." Kenzie nodded. "All of us. Without further ado, I dub Bree-Zee the speed demon of the Daredevils!"

Jules reached out and regally tapped one of Bree's shoulders, then the other.

"And I dub the Tomonater the blocking queen!"

Tomoko bowed her head as Jules touched her shoulders.

Jules swiveled to Kenzie. "And I, Crown Jules, dub you, Kenzilla, as the mastermind of the Daredevils!"

Kenzie waited to be dubbed, then turned to Jules. Shelly could feel her cheeks getting warm. Where was Kenzie going with this?

"Crown Jules, please dub yourself the ultimate bruiser!"

Jules patted both of her shoulders. "So dubbed!" she said.

And now Kenzie turned to Shelly. "Bomb Shell, you were the first one to see each of us as special," Kenzie said. "We've always been a team, but now, thanks to you, we're all superhero skaters too!"

Shelly's head dropped a little. "Is that what I'm being dubbed for?" she asked.

"No!" Kenzie brought her arm high. "I dub you, Bomb Shell, the creative genius of the Daredevils! The one who sees everything that's possible! The artist who flings a pencil like a sword!"

"I dub thee, creative genius!" Jules said.

Shelly closed her eyes. She imagined the Daredevils team spread across the track, and for the first time she saw herself like she saw the others. Shelly was the one who thought outside the box. She had the ideas that sometimes were just bonkers enough to work. When other people saw a squiggle, Shelly could see a picture. She was the one on the team who brought the impossible to life.

Jules brought her hand down on either of Shelly's shoulders. As her eyes opened, Shelly saw her dad carrying a heaping basket of tacos.

"Dig in!" he said.

The Daredevils didn't need to be told twice. They grabbed their fried avocado and Cotija cheese tacos and stuffed them halfway into their mouths. Bits of cabbage and cheese dribbled down their faces.

Soon the basket was empty and the napkins were stained and balled up. Bree propped her elbows on the wooden table and leaned in toward the others.

"Today was awesome," she said, "but we definitely need some new plans for the next time we go head-to-head on the track."

Kenzie looked up. "Mom! Dad! Can we go play at the park?"

The adults looked at each other and shrugged.

"If you've got the energy!" Kenzie's dad called.

Kenzie clapped and stood from the bench. "Let's go, then! Bomb Shell, can you make some sketches?"

Shelly smiled and reached into her bag. The five team-mates turned for the park.

"Let's race there!" Jules called. "Hot lava style!"

With her sketchbook held tight, Shelly took off along-side the other Daredevils. The hot lava sidewalk rolled out in front of them, oozing and bubbling with possibilities.

ACKNOWLEDGMENTS

The mantra "Teamwork makes the dream work" is especially true when it comes to the long and intricate process of coaxing a story idea into a finished book.

I remain everlastingly grateful for the three team members most integral to my journey with the Daredevils series. Thank you to my agent, Lauren Spieller, who advocates, cheers, and critiques at the exact right moments. Thank you to my editor, Courtney Code, who brings out the best in me and the best of these girls. Thank you to my illustrator, Sophie Escabasse, official coparent of the Daredevils.

Thank you to the teams at Amulet and Abrams, with special thanks to Marcie Lawrence, Amy Vreeland, Jenn Jimenez, Mary Marolla, Jenny Choy, Trish McNamara-O'Neill, and Megan Evans.

Thank you to the Albuquerque Roller Derby league for letting me take notes during practice. Go Unicorns! Go Narwhals!

Thank you to all my writing friends and critique groups—to everyone who helped me brainstorm, who left me alone to work when I needed it, and who cheered this book on from the beginning.

To my parents, Jim and Cymeon, thank you for the happy tears. To my sister, Brooke, thank you for leaving me fake voicemails as different book fans. To my dog, Sadie, thank you for keeping your side of the office relatively tidy. To my husband, David, thank you for being the *best* supporter and teammate. Finally, to the baby acrobat, thank you for sharing your mom with these pages. You've made my shiniest dreams come true.

ABOUT THE AUTHOR

Kit Rosewater writes books for children. Before she was an author, Kit taught theater to middle school students, which even a world-renowned cat herder once called "a lot of work." Kit has a master's degree in children's literature. She lives in Albuquerque, New Mexico, with her spouse and a border collie who takes up most of the bed. *The Derby Daredevils: Shelly Struggles to Shine* is the second book in Kit's Derby Daredevils series. Catch her online at kitrosewater.com or @kitrosewater.

ABOUT THE ILLUSTRATOR

Sophie Escabasse is the author-illustrator of the forthcoming graphic novel trilogy The Witches of Brooklyn. She lives in Brooklyn, New York, with her family. Find her online at esofii.com or @esofiii.